I Hate
to Talk
About
Your
Mother

I Hate to Talk About Your Mother

A NOVEL BY
HETTIE JONES

DELACORTE PRESS/NEW YORK

Published by
Delacorte Press
1 Dag Hammarskjold Plaza
New York, N.Y. 10017

Manufactured in the United States of America

First printing

Designed by Rhea Braunstein

Library of Congress Cataloging in Publication Data

Jones, Hettie.
    I hate to talk about your mother.

    SUMMARY: A teenage girl and her mother,
both with more than their share of problems, spend
a turbulent weekend at the Jersey Shore.
    [1.   Mothers and daughters—Fiction]   I.   Title.
PZ7.J7175Iah   [Fic]   79-53601

ISBN 0-440-04572-X

For my mother, who stuck with me,
And for my father and my uncle, who joined up

one

Alicia was furious. She kicked the suitcase up to the wall and then slumped against it, out of breath and overheated. They had run all the way through the terminal from the subway, because Fay kept insisting they would miss the bus. But of course Fay, being sick, couldn't carry the suitcase. Fat bitch, Alicia thought, I hope we did miss it. She looked up. The sign read WILBUR'S TRANSIT—8:45 TO BELLEMERE. That was the right bus, but there was no one else waiting.

Beside her Fay moaned. The smell of the exhaust was making her sicker. "Stay on line, I gotta sit down," she said. Tottering on her espadrilles, she headed for a row of chairs under the escalator and then collapsed into one of them, clutching her pocketbook like ballast against the nausea that threatened to float her away.

A red-haired woman passed and stared at them

curiously. Embarrassed, Alicia turned away. It
seemed as though everyone else in the terminal
were coming to New York, and she and Fay were
the only ones leaving. She glared at her mother
without sympathy. Anyone who got drunk over a
pig like Joe Viani deserved to be sick the next
morning, she thought. And Fay's hangovers no
longer impressed her, or at least not as they had
when she was small. Besides, she couldn't see any
reason for getting uptight. There was bound to be
someone else pretty soon; Fay always had boy-
friends.

But Fay was really feeling her age this morning.
Thirty-one wasn't twenty-one, she thought, and
even without a hangover it was impossible to keep
up with a very fast thirteen-year-old. "Did we miss
it? What time is it?" she asked, her voice thin and
weak as a baby's. (She never knew the time herself, she always asked other people.)

"Wait. I can't see." There was a clock on the
wall behind the escalator but the people coming
down blocked Alicia's view of it. They all seemed
unprepared for the suddenly warm weather: one
man with a terrible scowl on his face began pulling his tie as though he were going to choke himself. He looked like a shrunk-shirt TV commercial
and Alicia grinned at the sight of him. But the
heat was getting her too, and as she craned her

neck to see the clock, she could feel sweat gathering under the elastic that held her thick, curly, bunched-together hair. Usually she wore it braided and pinned up with a barrette, but there hadn't been time to do that before they left. She pulled at the wet mass now, wishing she'd had the nerve to let her friend Diana give her a haircut last week. But she'd been chicken: her hair was long and beautiful, to cut it was a big decision. She sighed, hating the problem, then took off her denim jacket; turning to lay it on the suitcase, she caught a glimpse of the clock over a short lady's head. It was only 8:40.

Well shit that's it then, Alicia thought, remembering that 8:40 was the exact time the last bell rang. So now it was really too late, and they would be just starting the volleyball game without her. Disappointed, angry, she slid down the wall until she was sitting on the suitcase, in a good position to hang her head and feel sorry for herself. Today, Friday, was a gym day; gym was one of the few classes Alicia had ever excelled in, some days the only reason she entered the school building. What a pisser not to be able to go, she thought, and also to miss the yard tonight, the weekend scene. Last night when Fay told her that they were leaving today for the whole weekend she had at first refused to go, then agreed only

after Fay cried and argued: "Why are you givin'
me such a hard time when you know how rotten
my life is? Why don't you wanna go somewhere?
What'll you miss—this?" Waving her wineglass at
the dark, narrow apartment.

Nevertheless, though saying yes was the only
way to shut Fay up at the time, Alicia had
planned to get up early and just go on to school,
knowing her mother was afraid to leave her alone.
But then having overslept she woke to find Fay
sober and contrite, apologetic: "Was I drunk last
night? I'm sorry babe, very sorry, we'll have fun,
you'll see, we'll walk on the beach and everything. . . ."

I should've just kept saying no, Alicia thought
now, yawning into her knees. She was not only hot
but hungry, in fact her stomach felt hollow, and it
didn't help that the entire lower level of the bus
station smelled of doughnuts. Coming out of the
subway she had asked to stop but Fay said no,
there wasn't time. And now of course they were
waiting. When Fay was drinking food wasn't important, often she forgot to cook or wouldn't, and
lately this had become more of a problem than
ever. Because Alicia's small appetite had become a
big one, her hunger immense, unfamiliar, and
nagging, and she was worried about it. And the
pizza and Coke she'd had at ten the night before

wasn't enough even then. She was about to tell Fay the time and ask if she could run and get something when the bus pulled in, a big green-windowed air-conditioned coach with SEATS 32 stenciled on the side.

Which struck Alicia as funny: why not 32 SEATS? "Look Ma, it's backwards," she said, and giggled.

Fay, coming toward her, smiled vaguely. She hadn't heard what Alicia said but was relieved to see her laughing. She found Alicia's anger hard to take: it usually made her feel so guilty and anxious that she had to have a drink. She climbed into the bus feeling much better.

The handsome, all-American type driver had short blond curly hair and a sunburned neck below it. After taking their tickets, he gestured toward the long carpeted aisle and said to Alicia, "Have a seat—ha ha—looks like you've got 'em all." She would have smiled at him but he was already looking past her at Fay, which made Alicia angry again, because it was a sore point that no one ever looked at her when beautiful Fay was around. Fay was blond and sexy and had once been a hippie although not very seriously. But she had kept a certain ease about herself that men always fell for, and she was also about twenty pounds overweight, which only added to her voluptuousness.

Alicia, on the contrary, was dark and thin. She had possibilities in the form of breasts and thighs, but she was thirteen and the only thing that had really grown was her hair. She dropped the suitcase and kicked it toward her mother, watching the dim interior of the bus. She felt like sitting in the back seat, alone.

"Where you goin', Alicia? I can't sit back there, it bounces too much." Fay was standing about three seats behind the driver.

Alicia stopped and half turned, knowing that if she didn't go back Fay would whine or get loud. She waited a minute, then stepped over the suitcase and kicked it toward her mother, watching Fay wince each time her foot connected with the canvas. (She knew there was a bottle in it although Fay would deny that, the way she did with the one in her bathrobe pocket at home.)

One last kick brought the suitcase an inch from Fay's red-polished toenails in the open-toed espadrilles. Alicia dropped into the opposite seat, determined at least to sit alone, and slid the suitcase in under her knees. Fay swayed uncertainly above her, as though the bus were already moving. "I'll put it on the rack," she said, guilty.

Alicia hesitated, then with a shrug shoved the suitcase out, then sat back and watched. As she had expected, when Fay tried to hoist it through

the narrow space the effort made her dizzy, and
she fell backward against the seat.

"Ma—" Alicia reached out to steady her.

"Here, let me do that." The driver loomed over
them, his long legs spanning the aisle. With a
mock groan he lifted the suitcase easily onto the
rack, then turned back grinning: "Whatcha got in
there—guns? Gonna hijack us?"

He had an unfamiliar accent, Alicia noticed,
like southern, or hillbilly. She watched him trying
to see behind Fay's dark glasses. Fay was just staring at him, unable to collect herself enough to say
anything.

"We'll be startin' soon," he said. "But since it
looks like you ladies are my only fares, I'm gonna
duck out for some coffee, okay?"

Fay managed to smile a little.

"Can I get you something?" he asked immediately.

"Some coffee please?" she said. She tried to
reach for her pocketbook without bending her
head, which was throbbing.

". . . and the young lady?"

Alicia frowned, mumbled "No thanks," and
looked away.

He stared at her for a second, then turned back
to Fay, who was offering him a dollar bill. He
waved it away gallantly and left.

"Why'd you say no? I thought you were so hungry," Fay said after she sat down.

Alicia didn't answer. There was nothing she could say, because the real reason was that although she loved her mother and thought she was beautiful she was determined not to grow up to *be* like her. Fay always let men do favors for her and buy her things, but then they turned mean and left her. Like Joe, who after half a year of presents and promises had abruptly gone back to Detroit. He dreamed his wife was calling him, he told Fay, he had to go. He had told her this on Sunday and by Wednesday he was gone. And now she was miserable and drinking. And I'm stuck with her, Alicia thought. For a whole damn weekend, shit.

The bus shook as the driver bounded up the steps. He handed Fay her coffee and then reached across to Alicia, holding out a large container on top of which was balanced a straw and a plastic-wrapped Danish pastry.

Alicia shrank back.

"I thought maybe she changed her mind," he said, with a wink at Fay. "You know these here young girls—they always say no when they mean yes."

Fay smiled at him and then glared at Alicia, who accepted the container with a reluctant smile.

It was orange juice with ice, cold and sweet she discovered. She sipped at it, savoring the chill. Then she sat back and unwrapped the pastry and took little bites off the edge while the bus wound through the terminal, crossed a few already steaming city streets where people were standing around squinting, and roared through the tunnel to New Jersey.

From the Jersey side New York looked even hotter; a white haze hung over the skyline. "Nice day to be gettin' out of there," the driver said with a nod at the city.

Fay pushed her glasses up on her head and looked out the window. "They said on the radio this morning it'd be in the nineties," she said, friendly, feeling almost normal after the coffee.

Alicia bit into the center of the Danish, which had both icing and jelly, but although it was delicious she refused to feel grateful. She had long before figured out that men gave her things only in order to impress Fay. She leaned back and chewed and watched them.

"Got a place down in Bellemere?" the driver asked.

"It's my boss's place," Fay murmured, feeling Alicia's disapproving stare.

"What's that?"

"I said . . ." Fay leaned forward. "My boss lent me his place for the weekend."

"Bellemere's a great little beach," the driver said. "I take my kids to the Fun House all the time when it's open. You ever been to the Surfside?"

"I've never been to Bellemere. Is it nice?" Fay was hoping to find a country house of the type photographed for *Ladies' Home Journal.*

"Bellemere's a hick town," the driver replied with a little laugh. "Though it does get better in the summer." He gave Fay a hard suggestive look through the rearview mirror.

Here we go, Alicia thought.

"It's hard to know about places," Fay said. "You know, whether they're safe."

"Well, anywhere you go someone always wants your money."

Fay smiled. "Well I have traveler's checks," she said, with the complacency of one who feels completely protected. She had bought them after seeing a TV commercial, even though the Jersey shore was only a couple of hours from the city.

Alicia sucked the last of the juice as loud as she could. Then she looked away and leaned her head against the window, wishing Fay could learn to keep her mouth shut, but knowing he'd probably hear her whole life story by the time they got to Bellemere, or at least everything about Joe.

The driver was saying that Fay's boss must be very kind and like her a lot.

Fay smiled sadly. "Yeah, at least *he* likes me," she said, directing her sad smile at the driver's reflection in the mirror. Sadness became Fay. It gave her a dignity she didn't normally have. The driver gazed at her as long as he could before turning his eyes to the road.

Alicia stopped listening, set the empty container on the floor, put her jacket over the ear that was closest to Fay, and turned her attention outside. She watched a man pumping gas in a green and white station and a pickup truck accelerating onto the highway. Then she pushed back her seat until she was almost lying down, and though all she could see was sky and the round fenced tops of oil tanks, it was so pleasant to be carried along in this position that despite being tired she no longer felt irritated. And the air conditioning felt wonderful. She lay thinking once more of how angry she had been last night, how uncomfortable, feeling as though her back would burn through the sheet. Fay says skinny people don't suffer from the heat but she's wrong, Alicia thought. She sat up suddenly, half asleep, and looked out the window. They were traveling fast, past rows and rows of houses and yards. Fay had moved up a seat and was having an earnest conversation with the driver. Right on Ma, Alicia thought. Then she lay back again, put the jacket over her head, and closed her eyes.

There was a loud noise in her ears. Alicia woke slowly, smelling the sea. She sat up. The bus was standing still, its motor off, the door open. Fay and the driver were gone. She ran to the doorway and stood on the top step, weak-kneed, her heart pounding, overcome by the awful fear that seized her whenever she woke and found herself alone.

The bus was parked in a gravel drive beside the highway, in front of a small white building. Across the road, beyond a cement wall, waves thundered onto a narrow rocky beach. Alicia forgot her fear in her excitement. It was beautiful, beautiful! She jumped off the step and went to look at the building. A green awning with white letters moved in the breeze; it said NORTON'S BUS STOP CAFÉ-BAR.

Fay's face appeared behind the screen door of the entrance. "Oh," she said cheerfully, "you woke up. We're just gettin' ready to leave."

"Leave? Aren't we in Bellemere?"

"Next stop." Fay came out the door as though to keep Alicia from coming in.

"Hey Fay, don't you want the rest of your

drink?" The tone of the driver's voice was loud
and familiar.

With a quick glance at Alicia, Fay called "no
thanks" and hurried up the steps. A moment later
the driver appeared, looking at his watch. Behind
him came two unsmiling men and a woman who
boarded, handed over tickets, then settled quietly
and separately in the back. When the bus pulled
onto the highway Fay left her pocketbook to sit
beside Alicia. She took off her glasses and stared
bright-eyed out the window. "As soon as we get
there we'll go to the beach," she said loudly, leaning over to give Alicia a kiss.

But Alicia pulled away. The smell of alcohol
sickened her in the morning.

two

Main Street in Bellemere was only three blocks long but it was wide, and there was a pretty grass mall down the middle of it with trees and stone benches and a monument.

Two assorted rows of buildings faced each other across the mall, like squatters under a high blue empty sky. Having been built at different times they varied in style as well as size: one-story brick boxes with plate-glass storefronts had been slipped between Victorian relics; beside a tiny real estate office (BELLEMERE BUILDERS) towered the blank closed face of a garage. The most modern structure was a bank with a sign that continually flashed time and temperature. When Alicia first noticed, it was 78 degrees at 11:48. All the stores on either side were gated shut except for the bank, a restaurant called Eddie's Lunch, and at the end of the street the Surfside Hotel & Bar, an old or-

nate three-story building that dominated everything else.

Alicia stood on the sidewalk in front of Eddie's
with her jacket over her shoulder and her hands in
her pockets, looking down Main Street while Fay
said good-bye to the driver. Just past the Surfside
the paved street ended. Then there were dunes
sloping down to a boardwalk and beach. On the
boardwalk a wooden building sat; a ramp over the
dunes led up to it and a faded sign that said BATH
HOUSE hung from its wide, old-fashioned eaves.

Beyond all that the sea moved green and shining, with sudden flashes of white foam. Alicia was
amazed because the beach was empty; she had
never seen an *empty* beach before, except in the
movies or on TV. She was suddenly very glad she
had come, if only to see that.

There wasn't much else. There appeared to be
only three people in the whole town. They were
seated on the mall benches and none of them was
moving. Alicia wasn't exactly prepared for this,
and the stillness unnerved her. As did leaving the
city anyway, for she'd spent little time outside
New York: the previous summer she'd gone to a
settlement-house camp for two weeks while Fay
found a new apartment; years before that, one
summer and fall that she could barely remember,
they had lived on a commune in Vermont—until

Alicia got lice in her hair and they'd come running back home.

The bus was parked diagonally at the mall, the driver on the top step leaning over Fay. This could go on all day, Alicia thought. "Come on Ma, I'm hungry," she yelled, and then giggled when the three people on the mall jumped at the noise. Being rowdy delighted her; when notes came home from school about it, she always replied to Fay's complaints by saying she liked to wake people up. Actually she simply enjoyed shocking them and seeing their various movements when they went to pieces (Fay especially).

It was stuffy in Eddie's Lunch despite two ceiling fans, and the red-vinyl booth felt a little sticky when they sat down. Eddie, whose name was on his shirt pocket, had three strands of black hair on an otherwise bald head and was almost too short for his counter. But the hamburgers he made for them were thick and juicy without being raw and Alicia ate hers hungrily, in silence, as though she hadn't eaten breakfast barely three hours before.

Fay watched her a moment and then grinned. "You sure eat more than you used to," she said.

Alicia stopped eating. "You think I'll get fat?"

"You mean fat like me?"

Alicia sighed. Fay was sensitive about her weight, but though she complained she never dieted, and when she wasn't drinking she ate a lot. Alicia didn't want to get into it. She finished her drink noisily.

"Stop that," Fay whispered. "You did it on the bus too. You want people to think we're slobs?" She tried to be very proper in public places, so that people would think her refined or, possibly, rich. In fact she had never been either. She was the daughter of a Polish-American fireman from the Bronx, and her sole venture into a life out of the ordinary had been to bear, when she was eighteen, an illegitimate, interracial child. Given the sixties climate Fay had carried Alicia off. But the seventies found her wanting a lost "respectability," while the child—whom she loved passionately— had turned out to be a born flouter of law and order.

Alicia looked across the room at the man behind the counter, put the straw to her lips deliberately, and sucked on it again.

Eddie grinned at her.

Fay reached for her glasses. "C'mon, let's go," she said. It was just like Alicia to pull a number, she thought, when she least needed any extra trouble. She jiggled her way out of the booth and paid Eddie but didn't ask him the way to Lennie's house, not liking the attitude she suspected behind his bland expression.

There was a policeman on the mall when they came outside, and they went to get directions from him. He was about Fay's age, dark-haired and handsome and unsmiling. Alicia disliked him immediately because he had on mirrored sunglasses; as he was talking she saw two reflections of Fay but not his eyes. And his unfamiliar uniform made him even more threatening; to her he was like a TV cop, and she had never expected to see one up this close.

"That's Lennie Moss's house," he said, after Fay had told him the address.

"Yes, he's my boss. He loaned me his house for the weekend." Fay smiled. She always smiled at the law, to Alicia's disgust.

The cop smiled too but his smile was only a gesture; it was impossible to tell what he was thinking behind those glasses. Pointing in the direction of the boardwalk, he said: "Make a left at the street above the beach. That'll be Azalea Place. But two-seven-one is way down the other end of it where the boardwalk ends, just about opposite the Fun House."

Alicia remembered the driver had mentioned a Fun House. "Is it open?" she asked.

"Not yet, miss, not for a couple more weeks. That's it, see that sign?"

He spoke with the same country twang as the

driver. He was pointing to an odd shape of gray wood, which was too far away for them to see clearly.

Alicia looked at his mouth, not wanting to confront her messy hair in his glasses, and mumbled "Thanks." Then she picked up the suitcase and started to walk away.

"Be sure to keep your door locked down there," she heard him say to Fay. "There's always vandalism around here out of season."

"Oh thank you," Fay murmured gratefully, as she was terrified of vandals, although her own daughter had been called that at least once. She flashed him a quick smile and hurried after Alicia to keep her from dropping the suitcase and breaking the bottle.

Azalea Place was narrow and rutted and ran parallel to the boardwalk. Architecturally it was as hodgepodge as Main Street: in between mansions had been built lesser homes, down to one-story bungalows almost dwarfed by complicated TV antennas. Large and small appeared unoccupied; many had shutters over their windows.

In fact no one seemed to be home anywhere. There were also no sidewalks, so they walked down the middle of the street, both of them holding the handle of the suitcase. Since Fay was three inches taller than Alicia even without her three-inch espadrilles, this was awkward. Then Fay took off her shoes, which balanced them better until Alicia insisted on removing hers too. Then the asphalt ended and they found themselves on a narrow gravel path. "Ow wait!" Alicia yelled after two steps. "Something's in my foot!" She sat on the suitcase and picked at her sole.

Fay wiggled her toes in the gravel. "When I was sixteen, I went without shoes for a whole day in the city," she said. "Me and my girlfriend Didi. We even went downtown."

"You went barefoot on the subway?" Alicia looked up at her and they smiled at each other for the first time in days.

With a nod Fay lowered her pocketbook to the ground and stood rubbing her shoulder where the strap had pressed into it. She was beginning to feel tired and a little shaky. "Didi stepped in dog shit on St. Mark's Place," she went on, sitting cautiously on the suitcase beside Alicia. "And for two weeks she swore she could still smell it on her foot!"

They laughed and leaned against each other then, both of them enjoying this momentary truce in the sunshine. It crossed Fay's mind that Alicia might someday stop judging her. And Alicia, loving Fay's casual sense of humor and affectionate nature, felt pleased for the second time that they had come to Bellemere. It was a lot cooler, she thought, and smelled a hell of a lot better than the schoolyard.

Two-seven-one was a short way up the path, a closed and shuttered bungalow like the others they'd passed, painted brown with white trim at the windows and on the railing of its narrow front porch. Fay kept saying over and over how cute it was while she fiddled with the key, although she had definitely expected something fancier. Since Lennie owned the business, she figured he was rich.

Alicia sat on the arm of a wooden porch chair and looked at the Fun House sign, which had turned out to be a laughing clown's face, his painted features almost hidden by a web of unlit neon tubes. As the cop had said, they were right behind the Fun House, but from the back it hardly looked interesting. It was the sea, the sound and smell of it, that attracted Alicia most. And that empty beach. She noticed a path between two houses across the street that seemed to lead directly to it. She was eager to get there.

Fay got the door open finally and they went in. The hallway of the house was dark and cool, and when Alicia shut the door behind her the air smelled salty, as though the sea were present even inside. She shivered and wiggled a little. The smell was intoxicating.

Off the hallway were two front rooms, one a bedroom and the other a living room. All the furniture was covered with sheets. At the back of the house was a single wide room, actually a closed-in back porch, which had small, old-fashioned kitchen appliances at one end and a narrow cot at the other. A door off the kitchen led to a bathroom with a metal shower, a cracked, sagging linoleum floor, and one of the smallest sinks Alicia had ever seen.

"It's kind of a cabin, like," Fay said, disappointed at the absence of white wicker furniture and everything else she had imagined.

"Hey man, it's okay." Alicia tried out her hustle on the square of gray carpet in the living room. Actually she liked it. They had never had a whole house to themselves before, however small. "But it's too dark," she said, and then ran around opening the windows and releasing the wooden shutters, which banged open against the outside walls. "Let's go out right away," she yelled.

Fay flinched at each noise. Almost from birth Alicia had tyrannized her with energy. But making the bed and unpacking her things took all the energy Fay had left. When she was through she took off her skirt and stood in her T-shirt and underpants, looking down at her fat thighs and thinking about Joe. "Son of a bitch," she said finally. "Why'd he do it? Why?" She rummaged through the suitcase for her bottle, took a long drink, and lay down. Lying down she seemed not so fat. Anyway fat or not she had a date with the driver, whose name, like his bus, was Wilbur— Wilbur Taggart. He had bought the franchise with a G.I. loan, he told her, after his return from the Vietnam War, and had named the company after himself.

"If it wasn't for war I'd never be a success," he'd said, shocking Fay, who had marched for peace. He also told her that he was married and a swinger because he felt it kept him healthy, and he wondered if Fay felt the same. She hadn't said yes or no. She did not plan to tell any of this to Alicia. In fact, she told herself, she was only going to have a few drinks with Wilbur Taggart.

Alicia finished putting on her shorts over her bathing suit and sat down on the edge of the bed. "Ma? You 'wake?" She shook Fay's arm.

"In a minute."

"You're not comin' out?"

But Fay was already breathing deeply, her large body relaxed and soft, a pile of pillows. Alicia leaned against her and stared out the window at a corner of the house next door, resenting that Fay had dragged her all the way here only to fall asleep. It would be stupid to hang around waiting, she thought, still she wished she didn't have to go out by herself in this strange, empty place. Given a choice Alicia preferred company, but she didn't get to choose much. It was Fay's life that moved them around, and especially since the previous September, when they had moved from West 81st to Elizabeth Street, Alicia had spent a lot of time alone.

She was tired of it. With a frown she got up, and after taking a towel from the suitcase crossed the hall into the living room, where beside the TV she found the house key, strung on a short length of white cord. She stood twirling it around her finger, unable to decide whether to take it with her or not. The door had to be locked from the outside. After what the cop had said she didn't want to leave Fay asleep in an open house. But then what if Fay woke up and wanted to go somewhere and couldn't lock the door?

"Well shit let *her* worry about it," Alicia said aloud, suddenly pissed off at having to make responsible decisions. She threw the key violently at the ceiling, but as she reached out to catch it a loud noise from somewhere across the street startled her so that she missed. She stood listening, a bit shaken. Then it came again and she recognized the hollow bang of a shutter opening against a wall. Pleased at this sign of life in the neighborhood, she retrieved the key and went outside.

three

There was no one in the street, no talk, not even a radio. All the houses presented their silent, covered windows as though they'd neither seen nor heard a thing. Alicia sat on the porch rail a few minutes, then crossed the street and walked along the path she had seen earlier, until she was among small fenced backyards. All the shutters in sight were closed, and there were no sounds other than wind in her ears and the nearby rush of the sea. It gave her an eerie feeling to be the only visible human among all those buildings, and she hurried on.

The path led up an incline behind the Fun House and then disappeared over the edge of a sandy cliff about ten feet high. There was no back entrance to the building, which extended both above and below the boardwalk. Alicia stood at the top of the cliff, considering whether to climb down and walk around the foundation of the Fun House under the boardwalk. Getting down was no problem—she was good at that—but it was dark under there, and the sand looked damp. On the other hand she hadn't seen another way onto the beach except the ramp at Main Street, and didn't especially want to walk all the way back there. After a moment she jammed her towel under one arm, slid over sand and rocks to the bottom, and then crept reluctantly into the dim space.

The boardwalk was only a couple of feet over her head. Beyond a half-open door in the foundation of the Fun House she could see a crumbling wood staircase vaguely lit from somewhere, and though it didn't seem likely that this was the way in, Alicia went toward it. But at her approach a faint sound came from behind the door—a rat? She turned and ran toward the sunshine and was just coming out when she heard another noise, even louder this time and directly overhead.

She ran onto the beach and turned around. Now that she could see it from the front, the Fun House wasn't particularly funny. It was old like the Surfside but not as elegant, and had been painted gaudy colors now faded. Pale red yellow green blue, it sat on the boardwalk with its back against the cliff as if it were tired after too many years of sun and water.

Still there was an air of welcome about it because all the shutters at the front were open. A
smell of wood hung on the salt breeze and some
new boards were stacked against one wall.

Excited, hoping to get a look at the inside,
Alicia ran up a stairway that led to the boardwalk
from the beach. Just as she got to the top a man
holding a hammer appeared out of the dark space
behind a second-story window. He had nails in his
mouth, and when he caught sight of her he began
gesturing and finally removed the nails so he could
yell. "Hey, git away from here, you," he shouted.
"Charlie told me to watch out for you—now g'wan
—git!"

Bewildered, for a moment Alicia remained staring at him.

But from the way he was waving the hammer at
her he meant business. She ran down the steps and
across the beach until her sneakers were so full of
sand that she fell. Then she lay still, listening, but
the yelling had stopped, and when she rolled over
to look back at the Fun House, he was gone. She
sat up and brushed herself off, worrying. Why
would anyone want to watch out for her when
she'd just arrived? Did she look like trouble? And
who was Charlie?

But her surprise at this development wasn't
long-lasting; Alicia was used to being chased,

especially from constructions. On West 81st that
had been their favorite game: she and Millie and
José Luis Vasquez had climbed over every fence
and scaffold in the neighborhood and usually
ended up running from outraged hardhats, like the
man with the hammer, and sometimes the police.
They did this not to be destructive but out of
curiosity and a desire for adventure, for they were
strong and agile and there were simply not
enough legitimate outlets for their energy—or at
least they knew of none, since they weren't allowed off the block.

But then they got caught. In Juvenile Court the
charges of breaking and entering were reduced to
trespassing, and they were released—with warn-
ings—to their parents. The experience had scared
them all to death. Mrs. Vasquez put her children
in Catholic school and Fay, on Joe's advice, had
moved. She never questioned Alicia about what
she'd been doing but had instead asked, "How
could you hurt me so?" thereby directing, as usual,
all the attention to herself.

Still all that had presented "trouble" as a very
real option; both of them knew that now and were
wary. After a few minutes Alicia stood up and
walked on, abandoning her hope of seeing the Fun
House inside. She wasn't exactly looking for any
more trouble—she had trouble enough this week

just dealing with Fay. And whoever wanted her away from there—Charlie or whoever—obviously had reasons. Playing it cool she took off her sneakers and walked along the beach until she was in front of the concrete foundation of the Bath House building. A chain-link fence surrounded it; she sat down there to watch the sea.

The wind had died down. After only a few minutes of sitting still, her neck and backbone were drenched under the mass of her hair. Impatiently she pulled off the elastic and wished she could decide about cutting it.

Fay wanted her to leave it long. "But it's so beautiful," she had protested when Alicia first mentioned this, shocked at any suggestion to cut the hair she had combed and braided so carefully, the hair she'd always loved. She also envied it, which Alicia knew and appreciated—gloated over, in fact—for there was some comfort at least in having long curly hair prettier than Fay's.

On the other hand a haircut would emphasize the difference between them, a prospect Alicia found intriguing. There was, she thought, the chance it'd make a curly Afro, and an Afro would damn sure tell everyone on Elizabeth Street the truth.

Thinking of this she fell back onto the warm sand, laughing aloud. A real kinky Afro, she thought, closing her eyes against the sun, could guarantee that no one would ever again think her Joe Viani's daughter, as Fay always let people assume. True, it was easier for Fay that way, more convenient that to all the Italians on Elizabeth Street Alicia appear Italian; Sicilian, Joe had said she looked, like the Mafia. She sat up and extended her arm. In the glare of the sun her color existed only relatively, darker than the sand and paler than the blue-green water, and she didn't know what she wanted to be, really. It wasn't that she didn't like Italians. The old ladies were always nice to her and said *buon giorno* in the mornings. And she'd had a crush on Paul Moscone since the beginning of school.

Still the fact was she felt uncomfortable with the very assumptions that put Fay at ease. "Just be yourself," Fay would say. Whatever that was, for so far she'd found no way other than the maybe Afro, and she wasn't sure about that either since her father, Eduardo Despres, was from the Dominican Republic. Which in New York, as she understood things, was about the same as being Puerto Rican.

She had realized this in first grade. Sent on an errand by her teacher, Alicia had surprised Roberto Núñez and a white girl from her block jammed against each other on the stairway. They

had both turned to her at once, their heads together as though in a photograph, and she had
stood staring at them, to their disgust, because
they looked so much like Fay and her father, who
had once taken a similar picture in a subway
photo booth. Years later, after Fay's drinking had
made her careless, Alicia stole the picture and now
kept it safely hidden, even though she could prove
nothing by it, simply because it was the only evidence left of Eduardo Despres. An illegal alien
afraid of being deported, he had refused to marry
Fay or sign his name to Alicia's birth certificate,
and had disappeared when she was two. Fay
could tell her nothing except that she had loved
him; that his disappearance had broken her heart;
and that in her eighteen-year-old innocence, she
hadn't realized how little she knew of him until he
was gone.

So though Alicia was half Polish-American and
half Dominican, the Dominican side was a blank.
During childhood that had automatically set her
apart—she didn't speak Spanish, or go to Sunday
School, or eat the same food as Millie and José
Luis. What she knew of life was Fay's post-hippie
existence: sex, grass, alcohol, impulse, and a lot of
explanations. It was a life you couldn't advertise
or export, although on West 81st your origins

counted less if you were skilled at climbing, and
Alicia was the best.

But now all that was gone, and though she half
understood spoken Spanish, and sometimes
dreamed she was speaking it, she was too shy to
try talking to the Spanish kids in her new school.
Fortunately the school was also a place where
mixed parentage, if not exactly commonplace, was
hardly remarkable, and the mixtures themselves
("mutts" or "all-Americans" depending on mood)
were accepted—partly because people tended to
accept you as what you said you were, since it had
become impossible to tell from appearances. What
could you call a black Jew—a jack or a blew? The
one who had a way with words (himself a "bop"
—a black wop) had dubbed Alicia a Polaminican.
She liked that.

So the move Fay had felt sure would cure Alicia
of antisocial tendencies had instead brought her
into contact with others who had similar problems
and ways to deal with them. She learned, for instance, the solitary materialistic pleasure of shoplifting, and experimented with sex and grass in the
empty rooms of the artists' housing project, a safe
place.

Still her responses to these new friendships were
tentative, and Alicia suspected it would be some

time before she could sort herself out, like with
boys for instance, and what she was going to become. Gym was one relief—a place of sure identity (*I am a girl, at least here that's what matters*)
and physical challenges that absorbed and pleased
her. Because to Alicia pleasure was still synony-
mous with adventure: pot was fine but it made
you sit still, and shoplifting lacked all but the few
thrilling moments between the counter and the
outside door. Now that the weather was warm she
missed West 81st, her lost paradise, and the ex-
quisite dangers she had known there.

A fly lit on her arm and bit her. Alicia flung
herself after it but it only buzzed away and came
to rest about two feet out of reach, ready to bite
her again, she was sure. She stood up and
stretched and shook out her hair to cool off. How
nice it might have been, she thought, to sneak into
the Fun House with Millie and José Luis, or even
just to go wading (none of them could swim). She
tried the water but despite the hot day it was cold,
so she picked up her gear and walked farther, fol-
lowing the boardwalk until it ended abruptly in a
broken set of stairs. Beyond that the beach nar-
rowed, then disappeared at a point of land from
which a jetty of piled rocks protruded like a finger
into the sea.

A round wooden building that resembled a

water tank stood on the point. A lighthouse, Alicia thought. It was old and crumbling and looked like a great place to climb into, and since there didn't appear to be anyone there who might run her off, she crossed the hard sand that led to the jetty and started up.   C881004 CO. SCHOOLS

The climb was more difficult than she'd antici- pated, because the rocks were slimy and held un- expected puddles of water. But on the other side she found a path to the building, which faced away from Bellemere toward the open sea, and was not a lighthouse after all but a small, rotting beach house someone had made an effort to fix.

In the doorway, positioned for sunbathing, was an elegant wrought-iron reclining chair, turning green on the remains of a grass rug. But though it looked inviting, Alicia wasn't sure whether to start back or stay. She went outside and looked around. The carpenter was working on the lower windows of the Fun House now, which she thought might mean he'd be done soon. When he's done, she said to herself, I'll go back along that path and wake Fay. Satisfied, she returned to the chair, spread out her towel, and lay down.

The afternoon sun fell right on her but above and in back lay a pocket of cool shade. Although hot, Alicia felt delightfully private. She considered taking off her bathing suit but thinking a boat might pass didn't; she never went around naked in front of people the way Fay did, partly because until lately any interest in her body had come from admiration of her agility, not her shape.

But all that was changing, not abruptly as her environment had changed but slowly and surely, and though she knew her body couldn't be stopped, her fantasies about where it would end were very disturbing. Even now there were girls in her gym class as large as Fay, thirteen-year-old girls with pendulous breasts that impeded their running. Girls who always lost, Alicia thought. She thought sometimes that if she could only see her father's body she might have a better idea of the possibilities in store: long or short muscles, for instance, large or small hands. Though he wouldn't help for tits. She pushed herself up on one elbow, pulled aside the top of her bathing suit, and squinted down at the flesh that rose from her breastbone and the brown nipple that ended it, hearing Fay's voice at lunch: "You mean fat like me?" Still she couldn't imagine the breast grown larger, what it would look like, how it might feel. Just as last year she could never have imagined her pubic hair and now there was a nappy black tuft of it, an Afro, and though she hadn't expected to like it, she did.

This troubled her too. She liked it all—the look,

the feeling, and sex was exciting—but she felt
these decorations on her body would enhance her
only at the same time as they slowed her down.
She didn't want to be fat and slow like Fay but she
wanted to be sexy. And she liked boys, muscled
ones especially, and liked making out with them,
the pressure, the loss of breath. Only last week she
had allowed herself to be ground against the wall
by Danny Crevit in the long subway passage near
school. And she had considered letting him really
do it the next time they were alone. Or when she
got more pubic hair. Alicia pulled the suit farther
down and looked at that too. It appeared to be the
same as last night, when she had lain in bed curl-
ing it with the covers over her head, trying to
drown out the noise of Fay stumbling through the
apartment.

But there were no such distractions now. Alicia
lay down again and let the sun envelop her body
until nothing existed except what could be heard:
intermittent hammering from the Fun House, a
motor scooter somewhere in Bellemere, and the
regular, hypnotic wash of the waves.

She didn't know she had slept again until she
was aware of feeling cold, and woke to find herself
curled on her side in the shade. She got up and

hurried into her shorts, checking in the pocket for the key and wondering what time it was and whether Fay was up and pissed off at her for having disappeared. She was so busy worrying about Fay that when she went outside all ready to go and saw what had happened it didn't register. She had to keep staring until she could force herself to believe that while she slept the point had become an island: the hard sand she had walked across was now flooded, and most of the jetty was a shadow under the water. She had no idea how deep it was but that was immaterial: she couldn't swim in *any* feet of water.

Alicia panicked. With a scream she ran back into the house and cowered against a wall. She knew vaguely that this meant the tide had come in but hadn't the slightest idea how high it would get. She was half hysterical with fear, convinced she might even drown, when she heard a motor and at the same time remembered hearing one before. She dashed outside again. There was a red scooter on the boardwalk, going the other way. "Help!" she screamed. "Help—I'm out here!"

Nothing happened. Whoever was on the scooter kept riding and eventually disappeared into the Fun House. She tried screaming again, but it seemed useless.

A chill calm settled over her. She found a spot

somewhat protected from the wind now blowing in from the sea and sat huddled in the towel, watching the rising water threaten some weeds, and thinking that it would serve Fay right if she died, or had to stay there all night or something, because it was all her fault, everything, even the fact that Alicia couldn't swim. If only Eduardo had stayed around he'd have taught her, surely he'd have seen to it, he was from the islands. Then she thought, if only he'd stayed in the islands I'd be somebody else. She cursed him for leaving his home to fuck Fay and make her, Alicia, and then go back home without teaching her to swim. Soon the pressure of her knees into her stomach caused a hollow pain and it occurred to her, as the tears started streaming, that she was hungry, terribly hungry, again.

Somehow that did it. She put her head on her knees and sobbed, cursing Fay, and swore that if she got off this place alive she would run away, she would do something. She worked herself up to a rage about it; Alicia was not one to die without a fight. When she heard the scooter start up again she leaped to her feet, wildly waving the towel in the air and screaming continuously, as loud as she could.

four

The man waded part way and then swam through the waves with expert easy strokes. Anxiously Alicia watched him come closer and then went down as far as she dared, thinking to help him climb out. But he did that effortlessly too, balancing on the rocks and pulling his way up until he stood opposite her on the path, water cascading off him in all directions and drops of it blowing onto her. "Gimme the towel," he said, without looking up.

Alicia shoved her towel into his hand, then stepped back to watch him while he dried himself. He was not a man but a boy of about eighteen with a broad, pug-nosed face and brown hair. He was short and muscular, attractive although not particularly handsome, and he was wearing a tight blue latex bathing suit with a round red insignia patch that said SHORE PATROL. She took another step back when she saw this, thinking he was a cop. But at the same time she also noticed with interest that surrounding the bathing suit he had very hairy legs and a long line of hair on his stomach. When he had finished drying himself he stood looking at her with his legs apart and his hands on his hips, openly annoyed at having to rescue her. "Damn," he said. "I thought you were the Crouch kid until I saw your hair."

Alicia reached up. The elastic had got lost and her hair was standing out windblown and enormous. She wondered how freaky it looked.

"What were you screaming about?" he asked. "Are you hurt?"

"I—uh—didn't know the tide was going to come in," she stammered. "This afternoon I walked."

"Well now you'll have to swim," he said impatiently. "You won't be able to walk it again until nine o'clock. Or maybe ten," he added, with a glance at the water. "The tide's run over two feet and Charlie's got us on alert tonight."

Alicia stared at him with no notion of what he meant and worried at the mention of this Charlie again.

He was staring at her too. "You're not from the shore, are you," he said after a moment.

"No, from the city," she said. "New York."

"You're from the city and you climbed out here?"

Alicia shrugged and was silent.

Then he said, "But you can't swim?"

She hated admitting it, especially to someone skilled. "I can a little," she lied, looking away.

"Well I guess I'll have to tow you," he drawled. "I'm glad you're not a heavy one."

Alicia could feel him studying her and quickly folded her arms across her chest to hide her hard nipples, which were pointing through the nylon bathing suit. But she wasn't about to be "towed" unless she had to, even by a muscular young man who seemed to be attracted to her. "Are you a cop?" she asked.

He gave her a strange look she couldn't interpret. "Not exactly," he said. "The Shore Patrol is Bellemere's private security force. But we've got jurisdiction over the beach."

"Oh, so you're like a security guard."

"Well, I guess so," he said, smiling. "Lifeguard, security guard, beach maintenance—I do all that." He paused, then remembered his impatience. "You can wear your sneakers but you can't take this," he said, handing her the towel.

Alicia looked with regret at Fay's best purple Cannon, part of a set Joe had given her when they moved to Elizabeth Street. Fay would have a fit if she lost it.

"Leave it in the gazebo," he said. "You can get it tomorrow morning at low tide."

"Where?" Alicia felt stupid asking. Then she suspected he might enjoy making her feel stupid.

"Ga-zee-bo," he said, as though she were deaf, or a baby, and then led the way to the building, where he stood looking up at the rotting roof. "This thing is an eyesore," he said matter-of-factly. "The town ought to tear it down." He took the towel from her and draped it like a shawl over the back of the chair, and then coming out tried to shut the door behind him. But it kept swinging open. He was so efficient and self-important that although Alicia was worried about the towel she was glad the door resisted him.

"Now listen while I tell you what to do," he said, after they were on the path again. Alicia gazed with horror at the water, which had turned a menacing dark green. The boardwalk seemed very far away.

"First what's your name," he asked, like a man filling out a form.

"Alicia," she mumbled.

"What?" He leaned closer, cupping his ear.

"A-*li*-ci-a," she said. "It's a Spanish name."

He looked shocked, then his face turned red.

"Okay, Alicia," he went on hurriedly. "Where-abouts are you staying?"

"Azalea Place, two-seven-one."

"Oh okay then, I can get you home," he said. "My name is Gary Willis and I'm a qualified life-guard, so you don't have to worry about drowning as long as you obey my instructions. Is that clear?"

Alicia nodded, but she was beginning to feel panicky and it showed in her eyes.

"Hey," he said, suddenly grabbing her by the shoulders. "Don't nut out on me, hear? It's not deep but there's a real strong undertow—"

"Get your hands off me." Alicia pulled away from him and started backing farther up the path. "Forget it. I changed my mind. I'm waiting here till the tide goes out."

"But I can't let you." He caught up with her and seized her arms, then tightened his grip when she tried to twist away again. "Listen," he said. "I don't know how you managed to climb out here but it's hard to get back, especially after dark. And I told you, there's a fog alert."

He let go of her arms with a guilty look as though afraid he had hurt her. He hadn't, but Alicia caught the unease in his tone, and the pros-pect of being stranded on this oceanbound island, in the midst of a fog, was like imagining herself caught in the hell Millie used to bring back every

Sunday from the Pentecostal church. She allowed herself an honest look into his eyes, which were serious and concerned.

"Okay," she said, unwillingly.

He smiled, a look of respect crossed his face. He was thinking she was brave, which pleased him, since he already thought she was pretty. He could tell she had been crying too, and this made him feel sorry for her as well as curious, for he sensed some difference about her. He didn't usually have these feelings for summer girls, though he laid as many of them as he could.

And he was right about climbing down, Alicia thought, after they'd begun. Although usually she could get down anything she'd gotten up, this time she had to be helped over the slimy, moss-covered rocks, which meant allowing him to hold her in various embraces until it seemed as if their bodies had touched everywhere—arms, hairy legs, hard pointed nipples. Even scared to death she didn't fail to notice this.

Finally, at the bottom of the jetty where water sucked around their legs in icy whirlpools, he wrapped her under his arm in some special way, holding her so fast she felt bound but not human, a package to be taken home.

"Now take a deep breath," he said, "and hold it, and when we hit try to let it out slowly. Got that?"

"Yes," Alicia whispered from inside the package. She was terrified.

"Listen, don't be afraid," he said. "Everything's going to be all right."

Then he pulled her along with him into the violent contrary darkness, the cold wet heavy suffocation. Struggling, Alicia gasped for air but swallowed water, choked, gagged, fought. But when at last he set her on her feet, his forearm crushing her ribs as he strained against the undertow, she gave herself up for a moment, let him hold the entire weight of her relief on his body. Which he managed easily. Then he dragged her onto dry sand near the Bath House, thumped her back a few times, and leaving her on her hands and knees ran to his pile of clothes next to the fence.

Alicia felt as though she had died and come back to life. When she had collected herself enough to get up and join him, she found him searching through his pants pockets. She stood beside him, shivering but otherwise all right, she thought.

"I need to get you a towel but I can't find the durn keys," he said. "Sit down."

"M-maybe you dropped them." Alicia remained standing and kicked through the sand around his shirt, automatically feeling for her own key, which was there, a wet lump in her wet pocket. Safe now, the key as a reminder, she began to worry about Fay again.

"Oh shit," he said suddenly. He peered through the fence toward the open basement door of the Bath House. "Oh shit," he said again. "I must've left them on the desk when I called Emily." He turned to Alicia, shaking his head. "You sure picked a great time to get stuck," he said. "I was supposed to be at the Surfside a half hour ago. And I *hate* climbin' this fence. There's hardly any space at the top to get over it." The truth was he had once got stuck, and it had been a very embarrassing episode.

"I'll c-climb it, I'm g-good at that," Alicia said, without even looking up, anxious to redeem herself though she was shaking like midwinter.

"No wait, don't, you can't—"

But she was already up, running vertically it seemed to him, and he watched open-mouthed. Although the fence was eight feet high, fences were what Alicia knew about. She got to the top, slid between the fence and the underside of the boardwalk, then started down the other side. Halfway to the ground she came face to face with his amazed stare. Then a phone began ringing inside.

Alicia hurried down the last few feet. "Should I answer it?"

"Yes—no, don't answer it, no—yes, maybe you'd better—" He shook the fence in confusion.

She ran through the doorway into a small room with lockers and a bare table. The phone was on the wall, and the acoustics of the room gave the ringing a loud echo. "Hello?" Alicia said. "Hello?" her voice echoed.

"Hello?" a girl said. There was a lot of noise in the background.

"Tell her just a minute," he was shrieking from outside.

"Just a minute," Alicia said, and lowered the receiver to the floor.

"If my keys aren't on the desk they're on top of the phone!"

The keys were hanging from one of the lockers. Alicia ran out, passed him the key ring, then retreated to the room, out of breath and shaky. Her hair was dripping a constant icy shower on her shoulders and down her back. The room felt damp and cold. She leaned against the table. Loud music was coming from the receiver. She looked at it wondering if she could get in touch with Fay, then remembered she hadn't even noticed a telephone at the house. "I'll just run home," she said to herself. "I'll get warm if I run."

The gate creaked open and Gary hurtled into the room, fully dressed. He yanked on the phone

cord as though hauling in a fish. "Emily?" he said.
"Em, I tried to call you before, but—no, Emily, it's
a girl that climbed the jetty, but I had to get her
off—that's the truth, Em, dammit—"

Alicia stood in front of him to get his attention.
"L-listen h-how do I get out of here?" she said
through chattering teeth.

"Wait a minute." He reached for her arm. "No
Emily, listen—" But the phone clicked off. He was
left holding the receiver and staring at Alicia, who
was now shivering uncontrollably and felt extremely weird.

"Now just hold on," he said to her in that peculiar hillbilly accent. He hung up, and after fum-
bling with the keys opened a locker and brought
out a heavy towel, which he draped around her
shoulders. Then he helped her onto the table and
made her lie down. "You must've had too much
sun," he said. "And I shouldn't've let you climb
that fence. But don't worry, you'll be okay." He
patted her shoulder and went away.

Alicia closed her eyes and wondered what was
going to happen next. She heard him rummaging
in the locker and then felt something being put in
front of her nose. "Here—take off your clothes and
put on these," he said.

She opened her eyes and saw a sweatshirt and
jeans but didn't move.

"You want me to undress you?" He was smiling.

"No," Alicia said, smiling back. "But why do I have to change clothes?"

"Because I'll have to take you home on the scooter," he said. "And you might catch cold."

He always took special precautions with city girls, whom he found inept and susceptible. Although this one, he noted again, was really different. He wondered if it was because she was Puerto Rican. He still couldn't believe she'd climbed the fence, especially after he'd nearly drowned her. He turned his back discreetly and busied himself inside the locker, pleased that by letting her wear his clothes he would manage to see her again.

five

When she had changed he turned and came toward her holding a bottle and a glass. "Now drink this," he said.

Alicia looked at him as if he were crazy. "I don't drink," she said.

"You're supposed to if you've had a chill."

"Oh." Alicia accepted the glass and pretended to sip it but the smell made her think of Fay again. She held the drink in her lap, as far from her nose as possible.

He sat down beside her on the table. "You know," he said, "you're the only summer girl I ever knew who crossed the jetty. How'd you learn to climb like that in the city?"

Alicia thought of all the times she had put chairs on tables in order to get her own breakfast while Fay slept, and then outdoors the scaffolding, fences. Nothing had ever seemed too difficult. "I dunno," she said. "I guess I just kept doing it."

"I never saw a girl climb a fence so fast. Isn't there something in the Olympics like that? Maybe you ought to train."

He was serious, and Alicia was so embarrassed she felt hot, and hoped she wouldn't sweat and stink up his shirt.

"If you're an athlete how come you can't swim?" he asked.

Alicia sighed. It was a sore point. "I learned a little once in camp, but my mother said the pool in our neighborhood was too rough so I couldn't practice."

"Well I can understand that," he said. "They say New York is real rough."

"Yeah, but now I can't swim. I really need to take lessons."

"Oh I could teach you," he said with enthusiasm. "You could probably pick it up fast. This month I give lessons weekday afternoons at the new Y in the Shore Farms mall. You should come." He immediately saw himself holding her, very gently, while her hair trailed behind her in the blue water of the pool. After everyone else had gone home, of course. A Puerto Rican Chris Evert or Dorothy Hamill, only a swimmer, he thought.

The idea turned him on. He felt he had discovered her.

"But I'm only here for the weekend," Alicia said after a silence.

"Think you'll be comin' back?"

She shrugged. This hadn't occurred to her. What was Lennie to Fay? Would she want to return? "I don't know. Maybe," she said.

"Oh." He paused, then continued, somewhat halfheartedly: "Well, there's a general swim tomorrow at the pool if you want to come. But I don't give lessons then."

His obvious disappointment pleased Alicia, but almost against her will. It was clear he already had a girl friend. "I'm sorry Emily got mad at you on account of me," she said, though she wasn't sorry but only wanted to say something nice to him.

He smiled. "Oh, I'll take care of Emily," he said in a knowing way. Then he frowned and shook his head. "But some girls will really tie you down if you let them." He glanced at Alicia and was pleased that her gaze seemed sympathetic. Then he stared at the cement floor, the corners of his mouth turned down. "I'm only eighteen, you know? I got things to do. Everybody in this town gets married out of high school. But I'd like to get out of Bellemere. It's too small."

Alicia, who had liked his muscles from the moment she saw him, began to like him even more for having strong feelings and being rebellious.

"Do you feel better now?" he asked.

"Yeah, thanks a lot." She stretched a little in the oversize clothes, feeling warm and comfortable, although hungry.

"Too bad I'll have to take you home on the scooter," he said, getting up. "Charlie's got the only car. Here, dry your hair a little more." He handed her the towel.

Alicia figured now was the time to ask. She began rubbing at her hair. "Listen, just who is this Charlie?" she said, trying to sound casual.

"My boss," he said. "The police chief, head of the Shore Patrol. Why?"

Alicia let this sink in. "He told the man in the Fun House to watch out for me," she said finally.

"Charlie told Roland that?" Gary frowned. "Well he didn't tell me," he said. "I don't know. But Roland's not from Bellemere. Maybe he thought you were Lena Crouch too. She's the only one usually climbs around here. Her grandmother owns the Surfside and she's a little—well, wild, you know? We sort of look out for her—Charlie does mostly. But if you come across her while you're here, steer clear of her, okay? I don't want to have to run around after the two of you."

He stopped talking, shrugged, then leaned over her. "It's still wet in the back," he said. He took the towel and pushed it around on the thickest part of her hair at the back of her neck.

To do this he had to reach around her, his face only a few inches from hers, and Alicia suddenly realized that he was doing it on purpose, and how easy it might be to get something going with him, especially in this quiet little room with the waves crashing outside. She thought of the times she and José Luis played under the covers when Fay wasn't home, and how quiet the sunny West 81st Street apartment had seemed against the roar of the traffic outside when they did it—or tried to do it. But this guy was grown. She was quite sure he could do it. And what if she let him—not Danny but a total stranger—and then never saw him again? The idea excited her, her heart began racing. She sat stiffly, trying not to breathe much until he finished.

He stood holding the towel and looking at her intently. "You know you're real pretty," he said. "You got the kind of good looks I like."

"Thank you," Alicia said, delighted, since compliments like that usually went to Fay.

"How old are you?"

"Sixteen," she lied without hesitation.

He lifted a strand of hair away from her face

and controlled his urge to kiss her. His passion for
different girls was driving him crazy and was one
of the reasons he kept deciding to leave Bellemere.
He felt so horny he wanted to jump her right then,
but he put away the towel and got ready to leave.
There was always tomorrow.

Alicia rolled up her wet belongings and followed him barefoot up a cement stairway into a
large room with lockers, and then out onto the
boardwalk. She had to hold the pants with one
hand to keep them from falling off. As soon as she
stood in the sun, she was surprised to feel her
thighs and shoulders burning through the cloth.
She hadn't expected daylight or heat, because it
seemed as if they had been in the basement for
hours.

"What time is it?" She felt a bit like Fay when
she said this, which made her start worrying again.

Gary shaded his eyes and looked up Main Street.
"Five fifty-eight, seventy-nine degrees," he read
slowly. "What's your house number again?"

"Two-seven-one," she said, trying to imagine
what was going to happen once she got there. She
knew Fay had to be awake and by six o'clock certainly drinking.

He helped her onto the back of the scooter and
then sat down heavily in front, kicking the motor
on at the same time. "Now sit close so you don't

get any wind and hold on tight," he yelled over the noise.

"Where?" she yelled back.

"Where what?"

"Where should I hold on?"

"To me, dummy!" He twisted around, laughing. "You scared to hold on to me?"

Alicia felt herself blush, but when her arms were around him his body seemed so familiar she forgot to be embarrassed; and as they roared down the ramp to Main Street excitement overcame everything else, for Gary was a joyrider, and he was intent on showing her a good time. He also, in the late afternoon shadows, managed to hit every rut in Azalea Place. To Alicia it was as good as being on a roller coaster and in a bumper car at once. When they arrived at the gravel path she was huddled against his back, out of breath and giggling, his T-shirt had slipped up, and her fingers were entwined in the hair on his belly.

Over the sound of the motor she could hear the TV blaring from the house. She climbed off the scooter quickly, hoping he would leave right away before anything happened. Once Fay had answered the door naked when she brought home a friend from school; ever since she had lived in terror of having the scene repeated.

But he was digging in his pants pocket, frowning. "Something's botherin' me," he said. Alicia, busy getting the key out, thought he was yanking at his crotch and averted her head. Then he pulled out a candy bar in a wrinkled wrapper. "I hate this kind," he said. "Here's a present." Before she could stop him he had reached out and slipped it down the too-wide neck of the sweatshirt. Surprised, she fumbled and nearly lost hold of the pants and her bundle of clothes, and by the time she caught everything together again he had turned the scooter around, and was laughing at her and revving the motor.

"Wait—what should I do with your clothes?" she said.

"Bring 'em to the Bath House tomorrow morning." Then he was gone, and the gravel settled back on the path. Alicia turned to go in. She was already halfway across the porch when Fay appeared in the doorway, wearing only underpants and a black see-through negligee.

SIX

"What's all the damn noise?" Fay said. She smelled of perfume and Scotch and looked frightened.

"It's just me—here." Alicia handed Fay the key and walked past her into the bedroom, where she collapsed on the bed, holding the candy bar. Thinking: Had he seen her tits when he put it down her shirt?

"I've been waiting hours," Fay said. She came into the bedroom and looked at herself in the mirror. Her hair was stretched tightly on pink rollers, which pulled the skin taut over her cheekbones and made even more conspicuous the circles around her pale eyes. "You're all red," she said. "Where were you?"

"I went—to the beach," Alicia murmured. The pillowcase felt cool against her hot cheek. She wondered whether the shower worked. The shower on Elizabeth Street never worked.

"Well, I'm glad you got back because I'm supposed to be at the Surfside at four thirty," Fay said.

Alicia hesitated answering. "It's a little after six," she said finally.

"Oh *no*." Fay stared at her through the mirror. "Goddammit!" she yelled, and burst into tears. "I could kill you for goin' off like that." She dropped the key on the dresser and stalked out, weeping into a shred of tissue.

Alicia lay still a minute, then got up and followed her into the living room. Fay was slumped on the couch, watching TV. Beside her on the floor were a Gothic novel, several magazines, a glass, and the bottle of Scotch. On one of the magazines, in bold lettering, was written: ". . . a man is what makes life worth getting up for in the morning . . . he adds the dazzle, the drama, the warmth to your life."

"Why didn't you tell me you had a date?"

Fay looked away, confused. "I guess I meant to but I fell asleep and when I woke up, you were gone."

"So why can't you go now?" Alicia said, wishing she would just do that.

"It's too late, he already went back to the city." Fay blew her nose with one hand and reached for the bottle with the other. "I just wanted to go out for a couple of drinks," she said sullenly. "It wasn't much."

"Then let's go get something to eat, it'll make you feel better."

"Nothing really makes me feel better." Fay sighed, shaking her head, miserable now with nothing to look forward to.

"But Ma, I'm hungry."

"You're always hungry lately, and I'm not hungry yet. We'll go a little later. Besides, you have to get dressed. And you should see your hair." Fay lit a cigarette and blew smoke belligerently at the TV. "And where'd you get those clothes?" she asked after a moment. She hoped they weren't stolen; she knew Alicia had been stealing lately but didn't know how to stop her. When confronted, Alicia always denied it.

"I borrowed them from the—uh—lifeguard," Alicia said, careful not to say *patrol*, which sounded too much like *police*.

"What did the lifeguard do then, go naked?" Fay was smirking. She loved to tease Alicia about boys because it made her own behavior less suspect.

"Ma, he got these clothes out of a locker." But she felt embarrassed anyway because *naked* immediately recalled the hair on his stomach and her fingers in it.

Fay focused her already blurred vision on Alicia, indolent against a chair arm, one shoulder out of the neck of the sweatshirt, her hair a mass of dark-brown curls. She looks like a porno ad, Fay thought, not without envy. "Well you sure look like you had a good time," she said. "Now go braid your hair—I'm not taking you out if you look like a wild woman." Alicia's impending sexuality terrified her. Suppose she gets pregnant and won't tell, or something, Fay thought, and then stopped thinking and drained her glass.

Watching her, Alicia sighed and slid into the chair. Beyond Fay and the flickering TV, at the open back window, a golden sunset filtered through the trees. There would be no dragging Fay out now, she realized, but she didn't really mind—maybe without Fay she could get another scooter ride. She was conscious of being naked under *his* clothes. She ate the candy bar slowly, with enjoyment, listening to birds call in the bushes outside, and watching the sky until it turned deep red. Then she went to try out the shower.

There was so much water that some of it even sprayed over the top of the cracked plastic curtain. She let it run on and on, lukewarm on her sunburned skin, and when she emerged finally the bathroom was misty and sweet with the aroma of damp wood. Feeling relaxed, her body enhanced by the sun and water, Alicia lingered, drying herself carefully and putting lotion on the burned places. Her breasts, now much lighter than the rest of her, appeared larger than they had before. She wondered again if Gary had seen them. She wondered also if he had gone to see Emily, and whether Emily had big tits. Then she put on her pants and sat naked to the waist on an old-fashioned twirling stool in front of the bedroom mirror, singing softly and making faces at herself while she dealt with her hair—which took longer than usual because it was so tangled, and she had to first brush and then comb out narrow sections, one at a time.

When it was all done she rested her arms and looked at herself critically, considering again the question of the Afro. Diana had advised "letting it go" after it was washed, to see what her hair would do naturally. What the hell, I'll just let it dry and see what happens, Alicia thought. Even without being an Afro it looked good spilling over her shoulders like that, setting off her dark eyes and eyebrows. It made her seem older, even, possibly, sixteen. She turned sideways and pushed her left breast forward with her upper arm and draped the hair over it. Then she tried out other, similar positions until she noticed that the wind coming in through the open bedroom window felt much cooler.

She put on a shirt and went into the living room, where an old musical comedy was in progress. The bottle, a fifth, was nearly half empty. "I'm going out to get some food," she said, turning on a lamp.

"Ish cold in here, thish place is freezing," Fay said. "Why'd you open all the goddamn windows?"

"Well put on some clothes, dumb-ass," Alicia muttered, remembering that it had always amazed José Luis how much she took care of Fay. Man, he said once, sometimes it's like you're the mother and she's the child. But that was the only way Alicia had ever been able to cope with the situation. She closed the windows and then found a blanket and threw it over Fay, who smiled at her in a vague sweet way, exactly like a child smiling at the mother who had made her more comfortable.

Alicia didn't smile back. Although she felt obliged to care for it, she hated this overweight, alcoholic mother-baby. It wasn't even Fay, and Fay was bad enough. After she had arranged the blanket she went directly to Fay's bag, pulling out first the travelers checks, in their neat blue plastic folder, and then the wallet, which yielded sixty-five cents in change but no bills.

"Damn that foolish bitch," Alicia said aloud. She picked up the travelers checks again and stood gazing at the blank line where Fay's signature had to go. Then she snapped the folder shut and threw it back in the bag and began wondering what to do next. Eddie's Lunch was most likely closed by this time, which meant going to the Surfside. With sixty-five cents. And they might not even let me in if it's a bar, she realized suddenly. Even with Fay's espadrilles on and her hair loose, there was no way she could pass for *eighteen*. All the good feeling from the rescue and the ride, the sunset and the shower, left her. She felt marooned again, the way she had on the jetty.

And not even Eduardo could help her out of this, unless he landed on the roof in a helicopter. She went to the bedroom window and leaned out to look down the street. There was one arc light a few doors down, but from there on only thick gray darkness with no moon. She hadn't imagined there might not be streetlights. She couldn't even see the Fun House sign although she knew it was there. The night seemed full of hundreds of dark possibilities, all of them staring at her lighted window, and she knew she wouldn't even go off the porch alone.

Alicia shut the window and then sat down on the edge of the bed. Normally Fay drank a lot but

functioned: she had been at various times a waitress, clerk, and saleswoman, among other things.
She also shopped, cooked, etc., and managed to
take care of Alicia even though arrangements were
sometimes very late or haphazard. But she didn't
stay drunk unless something happened, like right
after New Year's, when the company she worked
for went bankrupt and she lost her receptionist
job, which she had liked. She had been drunk for
weeks then, living on unemployment and hanging
out with Joe, while Alicia managed on occasional
meals and what she stole from the school lunch
program. She would have cooked herself, but like
tonight, getting money was a problem. Sometimes
there was nothing in Fay's wallet at all, not even
sixty-five cents.

But thinking about it now, Alicia wasn't sure
that if it happened again she could be satisfied
anymore with suppers of dry saltines and milk, or
that she would even stand for that kind of life.
Except to run away wasn't so easy: she knew a
number of people who had and most had eventually returned, or gone to live with a grandmother
or a favorite aunt. But she had no one to run to:
her grandmother was dead; her grandfather had
remarried and taken his second wife to settle in a
trailer camp in Florida while Alicia was still a
baby, and they hadn't kept in touch.

She hung over her knees, staring at the floor. And then there was money. Getting a job was out of the question—who would hire her for what? Some of the girls she knew had baby-sitting jobs, but on Elizabeth Street there were mostly old people. She had no idea of any other work she might do except go-go dancing, but although she could dance she didn't have enough tits or ass to make it worthwhile. And where could she live? The girls Alicia knew of who lived on their own had all been involved with stealing, or drugs, or both, and there was always an older man on the scene too. And then there was the last, crucial, question: what would Fay do without *her*?

Alicia rolled back on the bed and stared at the ceiling. She almost wished for Joe to come back to settle Fay down but then checked herself. "Fuck Joe Viani," she said softly. "Fuck them both." She felt thirsty and because the candy bar's effect had worn off, starving. She got up and went to the kitchen. Looking for a glass to drink from she found an open box of soup mix in a cabinet. Inside was one envelope with its corner torn, probably by mice. But it was still full, and there were noodles in it. She took it out of the cabinet carefully, so as not to spill any, and looked around for a pot.

* * *

Sometime toward morning Fay opened her eyes on the blue empty face of the TV. At first she didn't know where she was or why she was sitting up, and then after those answers came to her she tried to remember what had happened but got no further than sunset. It was cold despite the blanket. How did she get the blanket. Alicia, probably. Oh Alicia, I'm sorry, I fucked up, I must've passed out.

Feeling contrite made her sick. She needed to pee. She wrapped herself up and dragging the blanket walked barefoot into the hall. A light was on in the kitchen. Good. Alicia didn't like the dark.

Alicia. Where was Alicia. She said she was going out. Fear tightened Fay's throat. She crept through the dark space that was the doorway of the bedroom. From the direction of the bed came Alicia's soft, regular, sleeping-baby breathing. Fay turned away, relieved but still sick. What time was it, she wondered. Pitch-dark at the windows. She needed some air. She returned to the hallway and groping at the wall found a switch. A porch light went on. She pulled open the front door. Just at the edge of the steps fog billowed like smoke; long fingers of it reached toward her across the porch. She turned, tried to run, and fell into the hall with the blanket over her head.

Alicia, dreaming, awoke to the crash and the

blast of damp air. She sat up, unable to separate the squirming thing in the hallway from her dream. Then Fay struggled free of the blanket. Alicia groaned and got out of bed and turned on a lamp.

"I can't get it," Fay said urgently. She had part of the blanket around her and was trying to pull the end of it through the doorway, but it was stuck on the sill.

Alicia was used to Fay blaming her falls on chairs, tables, blankets, everything but liquor. She stumbled into the hallway and bent over to pull the blanket free. Only then did she see the fog rolling toward her, coming at her even faster than the water across the jetty. With a scream she slammed the door on it and dived under the blanket with Fay.

Trembling, Fay held her close, as much for her own comfort as Alicia's. "It scared me too," she said. "I didn't know what it was."

"It's a fog alert," Alicia said, hearing again the worry in Gary's tone when he told her. She shivered, and leaned gratefully against soft, warm Fay. Then she remembered she was angry. Leaving Fay in the hallway, she got back into bed and tucked the covers around her cold feet. "Go to sleep Ma, it's the middle of the night," she said.

"I *was* asleep—wasn't I?" Sick again Fay wavered, then dropped the blanket on the floor and went to the bathroom and threw up.

Alicia tried to go back to sleep but she couldn't. She lay with her eyes closed but was unable to control her ears, hearing Fay wash in the bathroom, hearing the floor creak as Fay came down the hall, the regular step that meant she had sobered up and was all right. Alicia sighed. Her concern for her mother felt like a weight she carried even lying down.

At last with a moan Fay came to bed, pulling the covers toward her side. Alicia, who had put all the blankets she could find on the bed, hauled the top one off and rolled herself up in it with a corner over her head. Still her ears picked up every sound. Somewhere in the distance a bell was ringing. She wondered how far it was from the jetty, then once more felt relieved not to be out there, stranded and in the dark. Fay turned heavily, emanating her perfumed warmth. Alicia shifted closer.

seven

It was still early Saturday when they got to Main Street and turned onto the ramp that led to the Bath House. The sky was completely overcast. A rainy day seemed certain; hunger alone had driven Alicia out of bed. She had dressed quickly and dealt with her hair as best she could, replying to Fay's questions about it with monosyllables and a stony stare. It was wild but she sort of liked that, and after a few minutes in the damp outdoors it got even wilder.

There was no sign of life at the Bath House except for a few indifferent seagulls on the roof.

"You sure he said to bring them here?" Fay asked.

"Uh-huh." Alicia stood opposite the entrance, Gary's clothes tucked under her arm, feeling foolish but at the same time relieved that he wasn't there, since Fay had insisted on coming along.

"Maybe he didn't come to work yet," she said. The flashing sign on the bank said 8:56.

"Well then we'll try afterwards," Fay said. She was anxious for her coffee and something to eat. She'd had one drink very early before Alicia woke up, but it had done little more than first make her sick and then to her surprise give her an appetite, which had increased as they walked along.

Alicia followed her down the loose boards of the ramp, hoping that later she could ditch Fay and come alone. Though the fog had dissipated, the only people in sight were two old men with canes, sitting on one of the mall benches. The bank was gated shut and Alicia had a moment of panic thinking Eddie's might be closed too. But it wasn't. Eddie himself, sweating below the brim of a hat that said NEDICK's, was frying eggs at the counter. "Good morning ladies," he said loudly.

Two girls in a booth at the back craned their necks to see who had arrived.

"Good morning," Fay replied in a polite but condescending way and with only a quick glance at him went to sit down.

Alicia, remembering his conspiratorial smile of the day before, gave him a big wide grin behind Fay's back.

"Not much of a beach day," he said sympathetically. "Said we may even have a little rain."

"How late do you stay open?" Alicia asked as she slid into the booth opposite Fay.

"We close at four thirty. You stayin' till then?" He winked.

Laughing, Alicia shook her head. "I just wanted to know."

"That's a strange thing to ask before breakfast," Fay said.

The little flame of anger Alicia kept burning at all times flared into the first fire of the day. "I want to be sure to get food later," she said. "Last night I ate rotten dry soup." She turned to Eddie, who had come out from behind the counter and was standing beside their booth with his order pad ready. "Can I have orange juice, scrambled eggs, French fries, and an English muffin with butter and jelly?"

"You sure can." He wrote, looking at Fay, who was still absorbed in Alicia's last statement.

"Er, I'll—uh—have the same," Fay said without thinking. "And coffee," she added hastily as he turned away. "I'll have the coffee now please."

Alicia pulled a napkin out of the holder and began to fold it into a fortune-telling game.

"Who gave you rotten soup?" Fay asked.

"You did, don't you remember?"

"Last night?"

Alicia nodded. This was her special torture, the best way she had found to make Fay squirm.

Tears threatened Fay's carefully applied mascara. "I don't remember that," she said.

"What's your favorite number?" Alicia was ready with her game.

Fay sighed. "Two," she said. "Honestly Alicia, try to be a little considerate. I don't think you realize how hard it's been for me these past few days, someone just up and walks out of your life—"

"One . . . two," Alicia said, working the game. "No luck there."

"Alicia?"

"Yes, Ma?"

"I'm really sorry I fell out yesterday, you know I—"

Eddie set the coffee in front of her and gave Fay a peculiar look when she reached for it with a trembling hand.

"Ma, when are we leaving?" Alicia asked in a low voice. "Can we go home today?"

"No!" Fay looked as if someone had hit her. She didn't want to go home, to face his abandoned underwear again. Even if it was a cloudy day they could find *something* to do. "We're not going till tomorrow," she said. "Tomorrow."

She sounded determined so Alicia gave up. "When tomorrow?"

"I—don't know what time the bus leaves."

They sat silent. Alicia fiddled with her game. When Eddie brought their food she asked about the bus schedule for Sunday.

"Don't think I know the Sunday run," he said, adjusting his cap. "I'm usually closed then."

"Well, how—" Fay cleared her throat.

"Oh you can get a schedule from Will Taggart, the driver. The Saturday bus comes down early, about nine forty-five, so he'll be here soon." Eddie gave Fay a little respectful nod of the head to show he bore her no ill will. He did, in fact, think her beautiful, but found Alicia's dark good looks more to his liking.

Fay brightened. "Thank you," she said, and gave him one of her tragic-heroine smiles.

Alicia, seduced immediately by the steaming plate, had already eaten half her eggs by the time Eddie left the table.

"Well at least I'll have a chance to apologize to him," Fay said pointedly, taking a very small bite of egg to see how it went down.

"Um." Alicia continued to cram in the food.

"Don't eat so fast, you'll get a stomachache."

"That's what I had before." She spooned jelly onto her muffin. "I only get sick when I'm hungry."

"Well it *looks* terrible, stuffing your face like that. Wipe your mouth—there's jelly all over it."

Alicia curled her toes tightly in her still-damp sneakers and reached for a napkin. Sometimes she wanted to kill Fay. Sometimes she wanted to just punch her out once and for all. This time she was distracted, luckily, by giggling from the back booth. The two girls had their heads together across the table, but Alicia couldn't tell whether they were laughing at her or not. Then the front door banged open and everyone in the store looked up at the driver, who was followed inside by an elderly couple in raincoats.

Will greeted Eddie and looking past Fay and Alicia waved at the girls in the back. "Hi Nita," he called. "How's your father, Emily?"

Emily! Alicia turned to get a good look and knocked her fork off the table. When it clattered to the floor everyone's eyes turned to them.

"Hey—Fay!" the driver said. "What happened to *you* yesterday?"

Embarrassed, Fay put down her fork and raised her napkin to her mouth. "Oh," she said, "I—"

He left his uniform cap on the counter and walked over to their booth. He had a hurt look on his face, only half contrived. "Hey, I thought we had a date," he said, loud enough for everyone to hear.

Fay looked at him over the napkin. "I'm sorry," she said. "I was all ready but my daughter took the key and left me stranded and then it was too late—" She widened her blue eyes. "I'm really sorry," she repeated.

Alicia would gladly have pushed Fay's eggs into her face.

The driver, ignoring Alicia, leaned farther into the booth. "Well do I have a rain check on that?" he asked. "I've already done my run. And Saturday's a nice, long day."

Fay smiled. She hoped he'd stick around, if only to rescue her from Alicia's criticism. "We'll see," she said.

"Be right back then." He patted her hand and went to the counter, where a cup of coffee was now beside his hat.

Alicia finished her food and sat with the balled-up napkin clenched in her fist, staring at Fay's plate, which had hardly been touched. "Are you gonna eat your French fries?" she asked.

"Here." Fay pushed the plate toward her.

"You're not gonna eat any of it?"

"I'm not really hungry after all."

With a disapproving grimace Alicia pulled out some napkins, opened them flat, set the muffin in the center, and piled the French fries on top.

"Makin' a picnic lunch?" asked the driver. He

was standing in front of their booth, with his hat
and his cup of coffee.

Moving in, Alicia thought. Remembering yesterday's Danish she tried to smile. But she ob-
jected to his line, and he was probably married too
since he had said he had kids. She didn't know
why Fay always fooled with married men. It
seemed to her that there had to be others. She
finished folding the napkins and wiggled out of
the booth, tucking Gary's jeans and sweatshirt
under her arm. "I'm going to the beach," she said.
As she turned to go she noticed that the girls in
the back were leaning out of their booth, clearly
enjoying the sight of this man they knew putting
the make on a weekend visitor, especially a sexy
blonde like Fay. Alicia moved to the counter, suddenly determined to fix their asses. "Excuse me, do
you know a guy named Gary Willis?" she asked
Eddie in a loud voice. "He works on the beach."

Eddie's eyebrows disappeared into his NEDICK's
hat. He glanced quickly in Emily's direction and
then back to Alicia. "Sure I know Gary," he said.

"I need to give him his clothes," Alicia said. "He
wasn't at work before when we went there."

At this Emily popped up out of the booth like a
puppet and sauntered toward Alicia on wedge
sandals even higher than Fay's. "Oh you must be

that little girl who crossed the jetty," she said. She pronounced little *l'il*, like a southern belle.

Alicia's whole body ached at the insult, but the way it had been put she couldn't answer yes or no, or anything else. All she could do was stand there and hate Emily and her tacky shoes that were one year out of style. What could he possibly see in her? Well, of course, she thought, tits and ass first, like Fay, only with brown hair.

"What is it Alicia?" Fay sipped her orange juice, staring at Emily over the glass. When people said things to Alicia she felt obliged to jump in. Despite the fact that her judgment was so off Alicia had told her more than once to *butt out*.

"Nothing," Alicia said distinctly, glaring at her.

"Gary's late because of the fog," Eddie said, breaking the silence. "He and Charlie were up most of the night, I heard."

"I'm a friend of Gary's—I'll take him the clothes," Emily offered, reaching for them. One look at Alicia's tight T-shirt and wild hair had convinced her that Gary was again interested in one of those weirdo types. And this one seemed to be almost like a Puerto Rican or something.

Alicia shoved the clothes higher under her arm and danced away one step, grinning. She knew *that* look. "S'okay," she said casually, in her favorite fake Nuyorican accent. "I jyust wanted to tell him thanksalot, j'you know?"

Total silence greeted this performance. Emily gaped. Fay's nostrils quivered and she stared at Alicia but was afraid to say anything for fear it'd get worse. Alicia rolled her eyes at Fay. "I'll just see if he's there now," she said in her regular voice, and walked out.

The street was as empty as before. The bank sign flashed 10:05 and then 73°. A car that said SHORE PATROL-BELLEMERE and had a long CB antenna was parked in front of the Surfside. Alicia turned and headed toward the Bath House, trying to deal with the lump in her throat, for as usual once her anger subsided she felt hurt and left out, and very much deprived of something that she needed, and although she didn't think it was Fay she didn't know what it was.

A fine mist hung in the air. As she walked it settled onto her, seeping into her clothes and her hair, which by now was shorter and wider than she ever remembered.

But she didn't mind the weather now that she was walking. Fay wouldn't have wanted to walk and good, Alicia thought, now she wouldn't have to. She could sit on her ass all day long with the driver to keep her mind off Joe. "And more to the point, he'll keep her big fat body off me," she said to herself, and was pleased with her choice of words.

Emily was a different story. Emily appeared to be a bitch on wheels and if that was his girl friend, Gary had bad taste. The only chilling part about Emily was that look, the first of its kind Alicia had gotten in Bellemere, the look that so clearly said: "I see you are *a dark person,* therefore I have grounds to suspect you."

The entrance to the Bath House was still locked. Alicia leaned against the door. Maybe he wasn't going to be there at all this morning. She decided to wait a few minutes, and looking for a place to sit down happened to glance up the boardwalk at the Fun House. One of the shutters on the top floor was open and a long wire had been strung from the sign in through the window. Not wanting to wait where anyone might see her, Alicia went around to the back of the Bath House and using Gary's clothes for a cushion, sat down underneath the overhanging roof.

The driver had said he was finished working, so there was no way to know how long Fay might hang out with him. In the city when Fay and Joe went out for breakfast on the weekend there were times they didn't come back until evening. And in the country a lot of people have cars, Alicia thought suddenly. She wondered if Fay would ever go off and leave her alone in a strange place with no money, and decided that if she got drunk enough she might but wouldn't remember later that she had, and then would be sorry, really sorry, like this morning. And like yesterday. But fuck Fay, Alicia said to herself for the thousandth time. The apologies never erased the movies her mind played over and over again, the memories of Fay stumbling, hung over, crying in the guidance counselor's office. . . .

Don't think about it don't think about it don't think about it any more. That was the sensible Alicia talking, who always took care of blotting out the rest of it. She leaned back against the wall, staring at the jetty, and tried to decide whether to bother about the towel. Not that there was anything else to do except wait, and she was too impatient to wait. She thought briefly of finding a way to go home but that was impossible. Besides, the beach looked different and interesting now. The tide had gone way out, leaving a wide stretch of flat wet sand littered with shells and seaweed. Everything was quiet, even the surf seemed muffled.

It was obviously the right time to go if she was going to go at all. She would have to leave the clothes though. Well, Alicia thought, disappointed, I'll leave them where he'll be very surprised to find them, and maybe catch up with him later, maybe at that place he said, the Y. But where was it? She couldn't remember.

She sat a while longer, watching gulls wheel and scream over the boardwalk. Then she jumped up and stretched and circled the Bath House looking for a way in. On the side facing the sea she found an open transom of opaque wire-mesh safety glass, which meant it probably led to a bathroom. Good, Alicia thought, bathrooms are always easier.

The prospect of a climb was all she needed to feel better. First she improvised a pack by stuffing everything into the sweatshirt, and tied the sleeves around her waist. Then she climbed to the hood of a ventilator and from there got a leg over the transom. It was a tight squeeze, especially her ass, but she had guessed right: directly under her foot as she slid inside was a metal partition. Alicia maneuvered herself onto that, swung down, and finding herself conveniently in a bathroom used the toilet. But a spectacular gurgling when she flushed it horrified her. She felt sure the man in the Fun House had heard it, and she cowered in the stall a long time before she dared to open the door. It turned out she had been in the men's room.

Downstairs the door to Gary's room was locked, which spoiled her idea of leaving the clothes in a neat pile in the middle of the table, as though they'd been flown in. She contented herself with placing them, department-store folded, against the door. Then she went outside.

On the beach the misty air was cool and pleasant, and there was so much to look at that by the time she got to the jetty the scene in Eddie's had faded into just another one of Fay's numbers followed by one of her own, and Alicia assured herself that she'd find Fay later at the Surfside, drunk no doubt but intact and with money, since the driver would probably be buying. Still she held on to the food package, for there was no sense taking any chances. When she found it hampered her climbing, she stopped to make two small parcels out of the one and crammed them, both greasy, into the breast pockets of her dungaree jacket. Then she continued, pleased that the climb seemed easier the second time. And the moist air smelled like a spring perfume. Alicia filled her lungs with it and then, feeling energetic, jogged up the path and in through the open doorway of the gazebo.

To her horrified surprise someone leaped out of

the chair and grabbed her. Alicia struggled and then broke free with a violent motion that sent her crashing against the wall. She slid to the floor. Looking down at her was another girl, whose fear seemed to mirror her own.

eight

"Who in the hell're you?"

"Alicia Prince," she whispered.

"You scared the livin' shit out of me," the girl said. "No one usually comes up here but me." She straightened up and backed away, zipping up her pants, which had been open when Alicia burst in.

Alicia stood up too, keeping to the wall while she brushed herself off. She didn't know what else to expect. The girl looked angry as hell. She was taller than Alicia, probably a couple of years older, and had a good figure. She was wearing jeans ripped at the seams, an old-fashioned blouse that was too small for her, and a pair of cheap worn-out sneakers. She looked weird but not dull or stupid. She had short blond hair, coarse and wavy, and her eyes were almost yellow, like those of a cat. Alicia was frightened of her and attracted to her at the same moment.

"You from the shore?"

"No, from New York."

"You're from the city and you climbed out here?"

Alicia nodded, remembering those were Gary's exact words.

"Is this your towel?" She had been lying on it in the chair.

"Yeah, I left it here yesterday."

"I saw you yesterday, sneakin' under the Fun House," the girl said, with a smile that transformed her face and made her beautiful. "I was under the old stairs. You almost came in but then you ran away."

Alicia frowned. "I wasn't sneakin' anywhere," she said. "I just wanted to go to the beach."

"Well you can't without a badge. You've got to have a town badge or get a ticket at the Bath House. That's why they put a fence around it." She sat down and lay back against the towel, squinting at her stomach.

Alicia suddenly realized who this might be, but couldn't remember the name Gary had mentioned. "Are you uh—Crouch—uh—the Crouch kid?"

She shouldn't have said it.

The girl sat up, scowling. "Charlene," she said slowly. "My name's *Charlene* Crouch."

"I'm sorry," Alicia said. "That's just what *he* called you, the guy from the Shore Patrol."

"Who, Charlie?"

"No, Gary."

"Oh, so you know *him*." She lay back, appraising Alicia. "He try anything?" It was a very matter-of-fact question.

"I only just met him yesterday," Alicia said, annoyed. What made the girl think she would tell her business to a stranger? How weird.

"Well, Gary's fast. All the guys in this town are. You gotta watch 'em because they blame it on you."

Alicia thought of Fay. "Well we're leaving tomorrow," she said. "I can take care of myself until then."

"You here with your family?"

"My mother." Alicia, relaxing, leaned against a table beside the wall.

"Watch out, that's broken," Charlene said. "I tried to fix it once but it didn't stay. It's the dampness." She closed her eyes wearily, as if more than the table had defeated her.

"Why don't they fix this place—like the Fun House," Alicia said.

"Because it's mine. The town owns the land but the gazebo's mine."

Alicia stared at this stranger lying so improbably on Joe Viani's towel. "Gary didn't tell me you own this," she said. "He just said your grandmother owns the Surfside."

"Yeah, Miss Thelma owns that and I own this," Charlene said, with a laugh.

"Miss Thelma?"

"That's what everyone calls my grandmother. 'Miss Thelma Rittenhouse Crouch, owner of the famous Surfside, formerly the exhibition hall for the state of Delaware at the Centennial,' " she recited.

"You mean the Bicentennial?" Alicia asked, because that word was familiar.

"No, the Centennial. *Eighteen* seventy-six. It was like a World's Fair. My great-grandfather had the building brought here and made it into a hotel. You had to be really rich to stay there."

Alicia stared at the girl's pale dirty face and worn clothes. She certainly didn't look rich herself.

"There's pictures in the Fun House," Charlene said, narrowing her eyes.

"Oh I believe you." Alicia edged away, put off by the flash of anger in those strange, yellow eyes. Charlene was obviously not someone to doubt.

"Where're you stayin'?"

"Azalea Place."

"You goin' there now?" She jumped up and followed Alicia to the doorway.

Alicia shook her head. She took the towel from the chair and stood folding it, staring at the sea. It had occurred to her that now she would either have to carry the damn thing around or find Fay and get the key, and she was angry at herself for not having thought of this. She looked at Charlene, whose expression was matter-of-fact if not exactly friendly, and vaguely remembered Gary's caution. But Alicia was used to relying on her own perceptions. At least there'd been no sign from Charlene of the hostility she'd gotten from Emily. "Are there any places to go in this town?" she asked. "Movies or something?"

"There's nothin' to do here until the Fun House is open," Charlene said. "All the kids are over at Shore Farms mall."

"What's Shore Farms mall?" Alicia asked, thinking of Gary but trying to sound disinterested.

"It's a shopping center a couple of miles inland from here." Charlene turned, working her nostrils in and out in an exaggerated way like a horse. "I keep smelling something, you got any food? I haven't eaten since yesterday."

Alicia hesitated, then reached into her pocket.

The girl really did look pale. "Here," she said. "They're probably a little messed up, but—"

Charlene grabbed the greasy napkin and unfolded the potatoes—a soft, broken mass. "Fries, great, thanks," she said, and began stuffing them into her mouth.

Watching her Alicia thought of black-and-blue Eddie Muller, who always took leftovers from other kids' plates and just disappeared one day from her third-grade class. She wondered if she'd ever get that frantic over food.

"Thanks," said Charlene again, when she was done. "Got a Coke on you too?"

Alicia laughed and shook her head, and didn't mention the muffin. Charlene laughed too, revealing small uneven front teeth framed by pointed incisors. "Well then I'm gone to get one," she said, hillbilly-like. "Want to come?"

"Where?"

"Around the point to the Surfside." She gestured vaguely behind her. "It's hard but you might make it if you got out here."

There was no doubt it was said as a challenge. In Charlene's eyes were little gold sparks of amusement.

Fuck you, sister, Alicia thought, and then said aloud: "Sure, let's go," although inwardly hesitat-

ing as the words came out of her mouth. Nevertheless she followed Charlene to a hill on the other
side of the point, and soon they were climbing
straight up, which wasn't bad in itself except that
the handholds were not as predictable as chain-
link fences. Narrow tree trunks, rocks, and
branches threatened to give way; there were thorn
bushes too and they seemed especially attracted to
the towel, which she had tied around her waist.
But rather than lose sight of Charlene she kept
going, and at last they emerged on a level, open
space that could have been a lawn once but was
now overgrown, with dandelions here and there
among the weeds.

"Turn around and look now," Charlene said.

With a gasp Alicia drew back and reached out
instinctively for something to hold on to, which
turned out to be Charlene's arm. They seemed to
be on a cliff overlooking the world, which con-
sisted mostly of sea and gray clouds banked above
it. Below and to the left of them lay Bellemere, the
houses like dollhouses, the cars on Main Street like
miniatures from the five-and-ten. Alicia felt as if
nothing but her own will kept her from rolling off
the field into space.

Charlene began to laugh. "Scary, ain't it?" she
said. "But I like comin' up here, it makes me feel
like I could spit on the whole damn town."

She turned and ran into the woods. Alicia stumbled after her but then stopped, stuck; a root had caught her pants leg. It was when she straightened up after getting herself loose that she saw the house, ruined and immense, farther in through the trees.

"Holy godmother!" she said (an expression first coined by José Luis). And it was appropriate too, for to Alicia the house might as well have been something that existed only because magically transformed, like Cinderella's coach. It rambled in all directions, bay windows and cupolas and trellises of decaying wood—but a facade only, for the entire back of the house had burned down. Weeds grew among what was left of the furniture.

"I guess these people were rich too," she said when she caught up to Charlene.

"Hell yes," Charlene said, in that twang Alicia still wasn't used to. "My grandmother's family owned it. They also owned a railroad."

Alicia peered into the woods and thought she saw another building. "Does anybody else live around here?" She didn't want to get caught in someone's yard if she could help it.

"That's the gatehouse where Charlie's family used to live but it's empty now."

Alicia opened her mouth to ask about Charlie but then closed it. If there was something going on between this girl and this Charlie she wanted to keep out of it.

Suddenly Charlene cleared her throat and spat violently on the ground. "Ugh, that burn smell makes me sick. I hate this place."

Alicia didn't like it either. It was worse than creepy places on TV, because TV didn't smell of charred wood and dampness. The woods were strange too, and dark even at midmorning, for the trees were old and tall and filtered out what little light came from the sky.

And the ground was again unpredictable. Like her trip from the jetty with Gary, it was harder going down. Several times Alicia had to slide on her ass, which was annoying: one of the few tastes she shared with Fay was a liking for clean clothes. "Are we getting close?" she complained, trying to rub some of the dirt off her pants.

"We're coming to it." Charlene didn't seem to notice that she was getting wet and mud-stained. She seemed lost in thought as she waited for Alicia to catch up. "There it is," she said.

"Where?" Alicia was looking the wrong way.

"Down there—" Charlene grabbed Alicia's chin and turned her face in the other direction.

The girl's fingers were strong, her grip tight, like that of a teacher or parent correcting a child whose attention had strayed. Alicia didn't like it.

She pulled away, noticing with relief a gray roof below them. Well good, she thought, I'll find Fay and maybe ditch this weird girl. She had also begun to feel hot and uncomfortable, and the extra padding of towel wasn't helping. She actually felt fat. She had to get rid of the towel—soon —or she knew she'd just leave it somewhere, and Fay would be furious. But after a few minutes they came all at once to a spring with a waterfall above the back of the Surfside. Just below them a series of sheds, with tarpaper and corrugated tin roofs, sprawled behind the original gray-shingled building. It looked like an elegant mother trailing poorly dressed children.

"When my grandfather was alive it was nice," Charlene said. "Now it stinks. Lookit the mess. I don't care if the whole fuckin' thing falls down." She bent over the falls to get a drink.

Alicia followed suit. The water was so cold she could feel it drop into her stomach. She drank only a little and then stood wiping her mouth on a corner of the towel, watching Charlene, who splashed water on her face and then awkwardly, self-consciously, tried to comb her short hair with her fingers. There was some improvement but not much.

She's got no style, Alicia thought. To Alicia style, as much as anything else, was identity.

What was on your T-shirt was important. She wasn't sure whether Charlene was suffering some kind of deprivation or whether she was just a hick. Either way, or for some other reason she only sensed, she suddenly stopped feeling wary of her and instead felt sorry for her. "You can use this if you want," she said, offering the towel.

But Charlene had her finger to her lips and was staring at the back of the hotel. "Shut up," she whispered.

Startled, Alicia looked down the hill just as an elderly woman wearing a faded housedress and leaning on a cane came out a back door into the shed area. She was stoop-shouldered and thin, with a tight mouth and a tight knot of gray hair at her neck. Alicia recognized her at once as the kind of tough old lady who calls the law if she finds you on her property. She watched silently as, using the cane to steady herself, the woman began dragging large and apparently heavy garbage bags from the door to one of the sheds.

Then Charlene signaled that they were to go back into the woods. Relieved, Alicia started to follow her but almost immediately stepped on a dry branch hidden under some leaves. It snapped in two with a loud crack. She fell.

"Lena? I hear you up there!" the old lady shouted. "You better come out or I'll call the county and tell them you were out all night again. Lena!"

Charlene stood in silent, obvious hatred.

"All right Lena! Stop playing cat and mouse with me, you little whore! *LENA!* I can *see* you!"

Alicia lay huddled on the ground, sure the woman was looking straight at *her*.

"You shut up, Thelma Crouch, hear me?" Charlene screamed suddenly. Then she went crashing down the hill toward the hotel, shouting that she had plenty to tell the county herself, about the lights and the water and some other things. She burst out of the woods still yelling, arms flailing like broken wings, and then the cane rapped her flat on the side of her head, across the ear.

There was a sudden, unexpected silence, as though the sound had gone off at a movie. Charlene sank to her knees, both hands reaching toward her head. The cane descended slowly beside her. Alicia tried to remain perfectly still behind the splash of the stream and the gulls calling overhead, but she could hear herself breathing and it sounded loud.

The old woman began to talk lower in a more reasonable tone; Alicia couldn't hear what she was saying. Charlene rose and still holding her ear ran up a metal stairway at the rear of the hotel and through an open doorway at the top of it. Thelma

Crouch watched her, then stood for a few minutes
with both hands clenched on her cane, looking
into the woods where Alicia lay. Then she turned
and went into the house.

Alicia stood up and brushed off her clothes,
cursing herself for having been fool enough to follow someone else into trouble. And the sound of
the cane hitting Charlene's ear had sickened her.
No wonder Gary had warned her off. Weirdos, she
thought. Let me get out of here.

She eased across the slippery rocks of the spring
and started down the hill, thinking *poor Charlene.*
There was something obscene about a girl that old
getting beaten. The last time Fay had tried hitting
her, Alicia remembered, was when she was eleven
and broke a mirror climbing to get the picture of
Eduardo. And then Fay had come home drunk,
and screaming about seven years bad luck had
started slapping her around. Until she hit back—
punched Fay, hard. Fay had never hit her again.
But there wasn't any violence in Fay, really. She
had certainly never hit with a *cane.*

Trying to be as quiet as possible, Alicia made
her way past the sheds to the driveway that ended
in front of the side door of the hotel. Nearby an
old twisted apple tree had bloomed. White petals
lay at the roots now, decaying but still sweet, an
overripe carpet. There was also an odor of stale

liquor that seemed to rise from the ground and seep out of the old wood siding. Charlene was right, Alicia thought. It does stink.

A toilet flushed close by, too close. She knew that if anyone found her she could be pulled in for trespassing. Main Street was just visible past some parked cars and a row of garbage bags and nested cardboard boxes. She walked down the driveway until she was beside the front porch of the Surfside and could look up the street at the bank sign. It was only eleven thirty and already eighty-three degrees. She turned and looked across the dunes at the still silent Bath House and beyond it to where the sky hung over the sea. The clouds were motionless, as though the weather had got stuck.

Alicia sighed and leaned against the porch. She was sweating. Her hair felt like a blanket. She took off her jacket and tied it around her waist, wondering if Gary was at the Shore Farms mall since he wasn't at the Bath House. But she had no idea how to get there. "Shit," she said under her breath. "Shit shit shit shit shit." She felt lonely and bored and burdened by the stupid loud towel, which she had rolled up and tucked under her arm, like someone headed for a swim. "Nobody in their right mind would carry around a towel on a rainy day at the beach," she said to herself, "how fucking stupid." All of a sudden she felt homesick for the city, where there seemed always to be someone else more conspicuous—shopping bag ladies, for instance. If only Fay had just *left* her there.

Fucking Fay, she thought suddenly. If it weren't for Fay I'd be high in the yard, maybe with Danny.

Having placed the blame Alicia immediately found a solution. Well fuck Fay, she decided (once more). Fuck Fay, let her hang around here, I'm going home.

It was a funny idea—running *to* home instead of away from it. She could take a bus or something. But there had to be money. She was trying to think of an excuse to get money and the key to the house from Fay when she saw the patrol car coming down the street. *Charlie's got the only car,* she remembered, and *Charlie told me to watch out for you.* For some reason Alicia felt sure he had really meant her and not Charlene. And now was she trespassing there in the driveway? After another quick glance at the car she ran up the porch steps and stood in the shadowy doorway of the hotel, hoping he wouldn't notice her.

Charlie Lovall watched her duck inside and for a moment couldn't figure out who had come to town without his knowledge. As far as possible he kept track of everyone in Bellemere. He had nothing else to do—his job was also his hobby, his lover, his wife. Then he remembered Alicia as the girl who had come with the blonde. Yesterday he hadn't noticed she was nonwhite, he thought. He wondered why she'd run at the sight of him, and something about her reminded him of Lena. He hoped she wasn't running from trouble because he felt too tired to deal with any, and was sorry he'd given Gary the morning off. He drove the car slowly up the ramp to the Bath House.

Alicia stood in the doorway watching the car ease onto the boardwalk, annoyed at herself because despite a clear conscience fear had overtaken her and she had run. She was trying to calm down when a sound came from behind her. Out of the corner of her eye she saw an arm coming, but too late. A man caught her around the shoulders.

"Gotcha!" he said.

And she couldn't move.

nine

"You looked like you were hidin'," the driver said after he had released her. He was in a very expansive mood. Noticing Alicia in the doorway he had remarked that she looked different from the day before. Exotic, he thought, like a gypsy or a foreigner. And he especially liked her little round tits and all that curly hair.

Alicia was shaking. It seemed as if everyone she met in Bellemere attacked her. After a moment she realized she was staring into the lobby of the hotel, a large dim room done up on a nautical theme: stuffed fish, shells, nets, and oil lanterns wired for electricity on the walls.

A bar ran the length of the right wall and ended in front of an alcove at the back of the room. Fay wasn't there. Alicia got out the "Where" of "Where is my mother" before Will embraced her again and announced in a loud voice that Fay had just gone to powder her nose but would be right back. The other people in the room—all men— were by this time looking with interest at Alicia, who squirmed out from under his arm. Powder her nose? she thought. Fay doesn't wear powder. Then she realized he meant she had gone to piss.

"Hey, McBride," Will said, reaching out again as though Alicia were no more than something slippery to be recaught. "McBride, this is Fay's daughter. Set her up with something, huh? What'll it be honey—Coke, Pepsi, Seven-Up?"

Alicia wanted only to say no, she didn't want anything, but they had been through that on the bus. Confused and still trying to see, she said nothing.

"Hell, Will, I'd buy her a beer." This from a long-haired young man with a hard round belly. The others laughed.

McBride looked up from his dishwashing and gave Alicia a quick once-over. "No booze fer jail-bait," he said. "Especially pretty ones. I wouldn't trust any of ya."

The men, including McBride himself, roared.

Alicia felt numb with embarrassment. She had never before been the lone desirable woman in a roomful of grown men. In the dim light she could barely distinguish their features, but she could feel all the eyes on her. The room was cool. Her nipples were hard and she felt like a fool with her jacket tied on. And that fucking stupid towel.

The driver didn't release her until they had walked all the way to the end of the bar, where over the back of a long-legged chair lay Fay's Mexican shawl. Alicia clutched its familiar rough surface but wasn't reassured. Then a door slammed in the alcove and Fay appeared, blinking. Alicia ran to her and for a second buried her face in her mother's fleshy shoulder. "Hi Ma."

"Hi babe." Fay hugged her a moment. She had heard all the laughter from the bathroom. She wondered what was going on, and what it had to do with Alicia's sudden embrace. She drew back for a second look, but through her two-drink glow saw nothing unusual except the muddy pants and the by now frizzy hair that they had already argued about. "Where've you been?" she said. "You're all funky."

McBride wiped the bar in front of Alicia and set out a napkin and a large ice-filled glass into which he squirted something from a hose. "She's the cola type I bet," he said with a wink, and got another round of laughter from his audience.

"Can I have the key to the house?" Alicia asked Fay in a low voice, trying to ignore them.

Fay climbed onto the bar chair assisted by Will,

who welcomed the chance to put his hands on her. "What's the matter?" she asked guardedly after she was settled. Drinking in the morning made her feel peaceful and nostalgic and she really didn't want to be brought down. Though it had always been that way. Every time she got something going with a guy, there would be Alicia. *Ma, I want* . . .

Alicia had expected Fay to be drunk but hadn't expected so many others to be watching. "Nothing's the matter," she said. "I just came to get the key so I can put this towel away. I don't like carrying it around."

Fay frowned at the purple velour, as intimate as her underwear. Like Joe watching her. She remembered walking in to him, naked, with the towel over her shoulder, and his comment: "Enter Fay Prince, naked, with purple towel," and then making love. . . . "What goes on," she said to Alicia. "What are you doin' with my best towel? This morning you just had that guy's clothes. . . ."

Will Taggart draped an arm around Fay's shoulder and drew her toward him, as though making apparent his claim despite Alicia's presence. But then gazing at the two of them, he saw for the first time the mother in the daughter, saw two women, not mother and child. Without intending to, he imagined them both in bed. He was delighted by the fantasy. "Hey, you find Gary Willis?" he asked, leaning toward Alicia.

"Did you give him back his clothes?" Fay teased.

"Yes Ma." Alicia looked away from them. She found it hard to talk to Fay when some man was stroking her shoulder.

"You haven't touched the drink I bought you," Will said.

Alicia took a sip to shut him up. The drink was so carbonated she immediately wanted to belch but held it in. "Gimme the key Ma," she said again.

Fay had considered allowing Will Taggart to take her home in a while and didn't intend for Alicia to be there. But then it occurred to her that Alicia might have the same intention. "What d'you need the key for?"

"I said. I need to put away this towel."

Will moved his leg a little so it would rest lightly against Fay's ass. He could tell the kid was bugging her. "Not much of a swim day, is it?" he said to Alicia. "And too bad the Fun House ain't open, then you'd have somewhere to go."

He might just as well have said, "Get lost so I can fuck your mother." Alicia's dislike of him enlarged, became rage. "I'm *trying* to go somewhere, man," she said, fighting an urge to do something to his smug red face. "After I put away the towel," she said to Fay, "I'm going to the—Shore Farms mall. . . ." Lies came easy when she was angry.

"Have a good time," Fay said. She lifted her empty glass and then set it down again on the bar.

"So lemme have the key so I can go." Alicia persisted.

"Leave the towel here," Fay said finally. "You're not hanging me up like yesterday."

Will Taggart hated to be around when women argued. "Listen hon," he said, "I've got some business to take care of." He went toward the alcove, leaving his uniform jacket hanging over a chair.

Alicia noticed a bus schedule in the jacket pocket. When Fay turned to the bar she snatched it, and then with her hand under her own jacket went to the bathroom.

She eased past a phone booth where the driver was busy dialing and let herself into the Ladies. It was a pleasant little room with a window through which she could see a branch of the apple tree. She sat on the toilet and smoothed out the schedule. It was hard to read; she wasn't familiar with timetables.

Will's voice came through the door. "Hi hon, what took you so long," he was saying. "What?

But I am talking loud, Lily. Tell the kids to turn down the TV."

"Leave New York," Alicia read. No, that was wrong.

"Listen Lil I've got bad news," he said. "Artie Reeves is sick so I'm going to have to make the four o'clock run.

"I know hon, I'm sorry too." His voice was tender, familiar, sincere. "So save me some meat loaf. Yeah, me too." Then he hung up and left.

Fucking lying motherfucker, Alicia thought. She found the 4 P.M. line under the LEAVE BELLEMERE heading. The New York arrival time was 6:51. She imagined the bus station at 6:51. It was gorgeous. The yard, where she would go, was half in shadow and full of familiar faces. She looked at the back of the schedule for fare information, but found only that they were subject to change without notice. She tried to recall how much Fay had paid for the tickets but remembered only a bill through the grill and then change passed back.

Fucking money, she thought, fucking money is always the biggest problem. She leaned against the toilet tank and stared out the window, watching the apple branch sway against the blank gray sky. Then she crumpled the schedule and threw it into the wastebasket.

When she came out McBride was attacking X-rated movies and Will had his hand on Fay's knee. It was a warm, sweaty hand and Fay could feel the dampness through her skirt. She felt so sexy she was a little short of breath.

Alicia sipped at her drink and was ignored until she asked Fay for money. "I need it to get to Shore Farms," she said.

McBride laughed. "Hey—you think you're gonna take a subway like New York?"

"Shore Farms is two miles from here on the highway," Will explained. "You need a car."

"And we discourage hitchin'," added McBride. "There was an incident last year."

"Why'nt you try askin' someone for a ride?" Will nodded over his shoulder toward the men at the bar.

The young one with the beer belly leaned back in his chair. "I'll ride you down in half an hour," he said coolly.

"I bet you will Paulie," said McBride.

That got a good laugh too. Even Fay laughed, which made Alicia furious. She sat grim-faced as everyone looked for her response to Paulie's offer. "I'm ridin' with a friend," she mumbled to him, then turned back to Fay. "Give me some money, Ma," she said. "Come on."

Fay made a great show of reaching into her

purse. She came up with two dollars, which she extended as though they were a hundred.

Alicia had been counting on five. "Tight-ass bitch," she said under her breath. Two dollars probably wouldn't take her anywhere.

"What'd you say?" Fay made as if to withdraw the offer.

"I said I'll see you later," Alicia said, taking the bills.

Whenever she had an audience, Fay went into her watchful-mother act. It was also easier to demand things when she was leaning on a man's strong arm. "When later?" she asked.

"I don't *know.*"

"What time is it now?" Fay demanded of anyone.

Several voices said, "Twelve fifteen."

Alicia hesitated, trying to think of something good. "Well how about five o'clock," she said.

But Fay wasn't finished. She leaned forward and put her arm around Alicia and whispered loudly, tipsily, in her ear. "Don't spend any money on him," Fay said. "Let him spend his on you."

Alicia grimaced and pulled away, then stood by the bar reluctant to walk to the front door past the lineup of smirking men. She wanted to scream at all of them to mind their own fucking business.

A red exit sign hung over another door near the

alcove. She ran for that. The door opened into an anteroom where a huge soda machine loomed, like a humming enamel sentinel. Beside it stood Charlene, a plastic bag dangling from her wrist, her foot in the open side door. Alicia plunged past her to the driveway.

ten

Charlene came out after her, kicking up gravel. "Your mother's sure fine," she said, and then gave a low wolf whistle.

"What'd you say?" Alicia felt angry enough to pick a fight with anyone.

A window opened directly overhead. "Lena, did you make those beds?"

Charlene ran for the nearest shed. Alicia hesitated a second, but she had no desire to encounter that cane up close. She followed Charlene into the shed and shut the door behind her.

The place was full of rakes, hoses, oil cans, and poisonous sprays. Charlene sat down on a low shelf in back. Alicia stood at the door, pulling on the handle to keep it shut and imagining it torn from her hand by Thelma Crouch or some giant in a uniform. Like Charlie with the glasses. *Did enter premises unlawfully* crossed her mind.

Charlene was perfectly calm. She sat on the shelf like a well-placed cat, smiling with her little pointed teeth stuck out. "Don't worry," she whispered. "She ain't gonna bother to walk back here. She knows I'll never make those beds."

Not trusting her, Alicia opened the door a crack and listened. She heard another window being raised, the clatter of silverware, and then from the bar Fay's drunk soprano giggle. She shut the door again quickly.

Charlene was grinning. "She sure got the hots for Will Taggart, huh? You shoulda seen 'em when you were in the bathroom."

"Listen, I don't like anyone talkin' about my mother," Alicia said.

"She fuck around a lot?"

"Shut up, goddammit!" Alicia bit her lip and turned away when she realized she had shouted. Besides, what was the use, people thought of Fay whatever they wanted to think. What did it matter what some crazy hicks thought? *Your mother fucks around.* She leaned against the wall and stared at the cracked cement floor, past images, past anguish floating before her. Edwin Santurce appeared chanting, on the stoop of P.S. 184:

> *I hate to talk about your mother*
> *but she sure got class*

She got popcorn titties
and a rubber ass

Anger filled her throat, threatened her eyes. Alicia pushed her face into the rough wall: *Don't think about it don't think about it don't think about it.* But the bar had overwhelmed her. The tears came and she couldn't stop them. She cried into the salty wood while the reasonable cautionary part of her brain told her you don't cry in front of weirdos in hick towns. And then that there must be something wrong, she was crying too much lately, it was stupid. But then she was *so sick* of peeping Fay's life.

Charlene had come down off the shelf and stood now with grave patience, offering a piece of paper towel. Alicia snatched it from her. It smelled like roach spray. She blew her nose anyway and wiped her eyes.

"Well at least she's alive," Charlene said. "I used to dream my mother would come back from the dead and take me away."

But Alicia was too concerned with herself to feel any sympathy. Besides, she couldn't have said who was better off. No, Fay hadn't died, it was true. But Alicia had been dragged everywhere, allowed to see everything, things she never wanted to see like Fay's white thighs in the air, a naked man jamming her.

And now, instead of being a little kid to be put to sleep on the other bed, she was jailbait. Fay was the same but Alicia was different, and conscious of it. That's why I hate hanging out with her, she thought. Everything possible with Fay they're going to try on me. Get me drunk and screw me. She wished suddenly that she could get that guy Paulie in trouble, or that awful McBride, to send them to jail for just one night. Then let them snicker. But she couldn't imagine herself enticing them; they revolted her, ugh, just thinking about it made her want to run.

She crumpled the paper towel and looked at the slice of sky visible through the partly open door. If only she could get out of Bellemere right now maybe Fay would never dare drag her anywhere again. "Goddammit, I really want to get back to New York," she said aloud. "I wonder how much the bus costs."

"Four fifty-eight one way," Charlene said.

Alicia hadn't expected her to offer this information with such assurance. But in the semidarkness of the shed, picking drips off a glue can and dangling her empty plastic bag, Charlene was again that odd mixture Alicia had first noticed in the gazebo and kept on noticing. "How come you know the fare," she said. "You ever been to New York?"

"Once or twice." Charlene didn't elaborate. She was glad she had seen Alicia's mother and all. She was usually the only trouble in Bellemere and she was more than pleased to have company. The sound of a large vehicle on Main Street reached them. She leaned across Alicia and pushed the door open, saying: "Let's go before the garbage truck comes."

"Where you goin'?"

"Shore Farms."

"I'll go with you," Alicia said. It wasn't going to be the yard but it seemed a decent alternative.

Fifteen minutes later they were still struggling through a wilderness of pricker bushes parallel to Main Street. "How come we can't just go on the road?" Alicia asked.

"I don't want to run into Charlie."

"Why not?"

"Because he *bugs* me." Charlene's face was expressionless. "The bus to New York leaves at four o'clock," she said. "You can get back in time if you don't stay at the mall too long."

Alicia shrugged. "It doesn't matter. I don't have the fare anyway."

"She didn't give you enough?" Charlene sounded surprised.

"No."

"How much did she give you?"

"Couple of bucks." Alicia looked at her without smiling, then shoved her hand in her pants pocket and closed her fingers on the two bills.

Charlene laughed, looking beautiful again when her thin nose widened and her mouth relaxed. "You're sure not like regular summer girls," she said after a moment.

"What do you mean?"

"They always have money. Most of the summer people who come here are rich, except a few."

Like Lennie Moss, Alicia thought. "Well not me," she said.

"Then how come your mother's here? She one of Will Taggart's swingers?"

"What?"

"He's a swinger. You know, orgies and stuff."

"Oh no," Alicia said, registering this.

"She doesn't have any money back at the house?"

Annoyed, Alicia stopped walking. "Look, forget thinking I'm rich because I'm not," she said. "In fact I'm poor."

"So then you really can't go to New York?"

"Not without money." Alicia looked at the back
of the bank, which they were passing. "Maybe I'll
steal some," she said, then tried to laugh it off because saying that made her uncomfortable. I'm
getting loose-mouthed, she accused herself. Like
Fay. The thought disgusted her. She stopped talking.

Above them the midday sun kept trying to burn
its way through the clouds. Alicia hated imagining what her hair looked like. They continued
walking until the line of stores on Main Street had
disappeared behind a screen of trees. At last, to
her relief, they climbed through a culvert and
then sat down to rest on a bridge across the access
road to the highway. Below on both sides of the
smooth asphalt the grass was green and neatly
trimmed, and the bright yellow center line looked
freshly painted. The road was a peculiar contrast
to Bellemere's rutted streets and old buildings. It
was the first new-looking thing Alicia had seen.

There was a sudden noise as an old Chevy con-
vertible crammed with teenagers turned onto the
road. The tailpipe was dragging. One of the boys
in the backseat stood up and spoke to the driver.
The car stopped. The boy got out and did something to the pipe. Then, straightening up, he saw

Charlene and Alicia. "Hey Billy," he hollered. "There's your girl friend Lena on the bridge."

Laughter from the car and shouts of "Lena!" as everyone turned around to see. Alicia recognized Nita, Emily's friend from Eddie's, who leaned over to whisper something to a girl beside her.

"Who's your friend with the hair, Lena?" one of the boys called.

"Is she another girl from Greystone?"

Charlene's face got very red.

"Oh leave her alone Ted," said the girl who was driving. "Come on Richie, get in and let's go or we won't get there at all." A wild-eyed, impatient-looking girl, she gunned the motor and put the car in gear. It started rolling. There were shrieks of laughter as Richie jumped in and slammed the door. Then they sped away.

"What'd he mean, Greystone?" Alicia said as she tried to pat her hair down a little.

Charlene's eyes darkened. "It's a school," she said.

"Oh." From her embarrassment Alicia figured it was a "special" school, so she didn't say any more about it. She'd known a few kids who went to special schools and they preferred to leave them out of the conversation. "They all call you Lena," she said. "Your grandmother did too. Is that your nickname?"

"My name's Charlene," she said, frowning.

Alicia didn't press it. "Too bad we couldn't get a ride," she said to change the subject.

"Ah, they never want to hang around with me."

"How come?"

"Because of Miss Thelma and everything." Charlene shrugged. "Trouble, you know." She pointed to her ear.

Alicia sat looking at the tight, angry mouth (like her grandmother's), thinking maybe she should say good-bye and go somewhere to wait for Fay until five. But where? Unless she got hold of some money she wasn't going to New York until tomorrow. "Okay Charlene, let's go," she said by way of a truce, and stood up, stretching.

"It's a two-mile walk." Charlene's grinning challenge was familiar this time.

"I know that," Alicia said. "And you're not supposed to hitch. They told me in the bar."

Charlene nodded. "Maggie DeMiola got a ride from some guy who had a gun. He took her all the way up to Asbury and made her suck it."

"The gun?" sophisticated Alicia said, laughing.

For a moment Charlene looked puzzled. Then she laughed, a hearty hillbilly kind of guffaw, and they headed toward the highway.

eleven

The highway traffic scared her more than the cars
in New York. City drivers were at least afraid to
kill you, Alicia thought, and drove slow enough to
blow kisses or curse you out if you got in the way.
But here they passed with a blast of sound and
heat, and seemed horrified by the sight of two
girls walking, as though pedestrians couldn't exist
on highways. Alicia felt alien enough without that
hostility. She began to see that *hick* depended on
where you were; in this place she was the one to
watch. It made her nervous.

Though she liked walking with Charlene. It
wasn't often she met a girl who could keep a steady
pace. Millie, for instance, had to run to keep up,
and Fay's balance was always off. But Charlene
traveled at exactly the right speed. Alicia sensed
she felt this too, for though they didn't talk much,

from time to time they smiled at each other, especially when cars passed.

Nevertheless after a mile on the graveled shoulder she was glad when they came to a rest stop. She followed Charlene past a few picnic tables and a rusted garbage barrel, and then along a path to a pond that materialized all at once through the trees. When they emerged on the shore, some ducks skittered to the far end. Quacking, Alicia supposed, though it didn't really sound like that.

"They'll stay—they have babies," Charlene said softly.

A large duck with a green-and-blue-feathered head swam back and forth in front of the others, presenting to them first one, then the other glittering eye. "He's the father," Charlene said.

"How do you know?"

"They're the ones with the colors. The females are always plain brown."

Alicia regarded the ducks thoughtfully as she took off her sneakers, feeling like an intruder and vaguely annoyed at the female duck for not having beautiful colors. She waded after Charlene to the far shore, where they sat down in front of a tree near a pile of blackened stones that still smelled like fire. Alicia immediately remembered the burned house on the hill and the thought spooked her. But after a few minutes the ducks calmed down and began to swim around again and she relaxed too. She leaned back, wiggling her toes in the humid air, glad to be barefoot and sitting.

Charlene was also propped against the tree, on the other side of a huge root. She put her bare foot against Alicia's.

"Your feet are bigger than mine even though you're smaller," she said.

Alicia laughed. "Yeah, I got big feet," she said. "I can wear my mother's shoes and she's three inches taller than me. But our feet are completely different," she added. Alicia always denied any physical resemblance to Fay. "She thinks mine are sort of like my father's but not exactly."

"What are your father's like?"

"I never saw them," Alicia said, surprised to find herself able to say that so easily. "I have a picture of his face but not his feet."

Charlene was silent, reacting to this. "I hate my feet," she said after a while. "My toes look like white worms. At least you got a good tan on yours."

"That's my natural color," Alicia said mildly.

"Are you *colored*?" Charlene twisted around the root to squint at her.

"I'm half Polish-American and half Dominican."
Alicia stared her down, thinking she could decide
for herself what color that was.

"But what's a Dominican?"

"A person from the Dominican Republic, from
the islands. Like Puerto Rico," she prompted,
when Charlene still looked blank.

"Oh, you're Puerto *Rican*."

"No, Polaminican." She laughed.

Charlene frowned, still confused. "Well anyway, you're half American whatever it is, right?"
Alicia nodded.

Charlene settled back. "I'm only half Crouch,"
she said, after a silence. "That makes me the same
as you."

The statement was meaningless to Alicia. Being
half something had no consequences if you were
all white. "What's your other half?" she asked
anyway.

Charlene sat up suddenly, grabbed her arm
hard, and held on. "You won't tell?"

"Hey, what is this shit? Lemme go!"

"You won't tell Gary Willis?"

"No I won't tell him—okay?" Alicia pried her
arm free. She doubted she'd see Gary again anyway. Whenever she chased boys she usually
missed them. She moved farther away from Char-

lene. "And from now on keep your hands off me," she said. "I don't like being grabbed."

Charlene's eyes darkened but she didn't apologize. She leaned on the root, digging at a half-buried stone. "You saw everyone calls me Lena," she said. "Lena, Lena, Lena, Lena. I *hate* that name." She got the stone free and threw it violently into the pond. The ducks scattered squawking.

Alicia waited, ready to run, but when Charlene continued her voice was calm. "Lena was my grandmother's idea; it's short for Helene."

"Is Helene your real name?"

"*Char*lene's my name, after Charlie. He's my father, but nobody knows. Helene was my mother, my fucking dead whore of a mother, you know?"

"Jesus," Alicia whispered under her breath. She stared at Charlene's taut profile, frightened by her violence and changeability but drawn by the strength of that anger, which she respected. It made her own seem almost casual. "So how'd you find out if nobody knows?" she asked. She made it a point to collect found-father stories, but this one was vague.

"You don't believe me?"

"Well how do you know for sure?"

For a moment Charlene looked confused. "Oh I

been thinkin' about it a long time now, and in my heart I know that's who I am," she said slowly. "Everyone thinks he's always after me because his family used to be my grandmother's servants. But when he drove me home the last time I saw our eyes are exactly the same, that's why he always wears those glasses."

Charlie, the cop in the car. Alicia tried to recall whether he looked like Charlene but could only remember the mirrored glasses and that he was handsome. But then she thought it didn't matter, that even if she didn't believe Charlene, she should honor what Charlene wanted to be. She picked up a stick and began to peel the bark from it. "So what's gonna happen?" she asked. "You think you'll ever get it together?"

"Nah, he's chickenshit," Charlene said, shaking her head back and forth several times as if more than one negative were needed to express what she felt. "Because if he *really* loved me . . ."

At least he could keep her from getting beat up. Alicia stirred the campfire ashes with her stick, wondering suddenly if Eduardo could ever *really* love her, enough, that is, to rescue her from some intolerable situation. She supposed she'd have to go to the Dominican Republic to find out. She saw herself on a plane, flying to find him. But the image was hazy. She would have to be beautiful though, and hip. She thought of the poster on the wall at the corner of Elizabeth and Houston streets, for Movimiento Popular Dominicano. The person in the poster—a man or woman she couldn't tell—had hair sort of straight, like Freddie Prinze's. Maybe an Afro wasn't the answer, she thought. Eduardo had an Afro in the picture, but did he have one now? Alicia usually thought of him only in relation to her own image, of how he was part of her; she couldn't picture him now because he was just too far away to exist. It must be different with Charlene and Charlie, she thought enviously. Charlie was *real*. "You're not even gonna say anything to him?" she asked.

"I'm leavin' town." Charlene began to run her fingers through her hair in a nervous repetitive gesture. "I just want to go where no one knows me, or my family."

"I always wished I had a family," Alicia said.

Charlene laughed. For as long as she could remember the Crouch in her had meant misery and isolation. "You wouldn't want one if it's gone downhill," she said. "I finished it, that's what my grandmother says, I'm the end. I'm too awkward for a Rittenhouse and too stupid for a Crouch, she says, and I have peasant bones.

"But she's the bony one," Charlene went on. "She's a dead person who's still alive. She'll call the county on me but I'm gone, I tell you this time I'm gone."

The speech seemed to have exhausted her. She closed her eyes and fell back against the tree. She still looked unnaturally pale, and moved her head stiffly.

Her ear probably hurts, Alicia thought, feeling sorry for her again. "Wow," she said, "that's a heavy trip, man."

Charlene glanced up. "You ever run away?"

"I never have money. It's expensive taking care of yourself, at least in New York it is."

"I can get a job in Asbury whenever I want," Charlene said. "Dancing."

"Topless?"

She shrugged. "I ain't done it yet. Mr. Hatch just promised me last night, I mean Manny." She giggled, and color flooded her face, making her look almost healthy. "He's in Bellemere Builders," she explained.

"That store on Main Street?"

"They got another one in Shore Farms. It's a real estate company. They own a lot of things. He wants to buy the Surfside too but my grandmother won't sell it. Although she sold my land to the town." Charlene grimaced. "Where the gazebo is. My grandfather always told me that was mine."

"How come she won't sell the Surfside too?" Alicia thought of the strain on Thelma Crouch's face as she hauled the garbage bags.

"She says if she sells it they'll ruin it, it's her duty to keep it. But the Council wants Hatch to put Bellemere on the map. They say she's holding the town back. It's their town, they say, not just one family's. And she don't even know what goes on there already. McBride and them, they do all kind of stuff behind her back."

Alicia thought immediately of Fay and Will Taggart's orgies, and a knot of concern began in her belly. "Well who do you agree with about the Surfside?" she asked, trying to force the Fay-thoughts away.

Charlene stared at the ducks. "I never can make up my mind. I try to but it drives me crazy. Hatch says he'd fix the bar up nice, with colored lights and all, and get some girls in to dance." She looked down at herself. "He says I got a good body for dancing."

"Can you dance?"

"Nah." She he-hawed. "Can you?"

"Yeah, but I don't have—"

"You got *hair*." Charlene scrambled over the root and knelt in front of Alicia. "See, you can hang it down in front, it'll hide—"

She had her hands in Alicia's hair and was tugging hard, pulling it around Alicia's face and down her shoulders toward her breasts.

"Jesus Christ, let *go!*" Alicia brought her arms up through center and pushed out, unbalancing Charlene, who stumbled backward and almost fell in the pond. She slid to a stop, grasping the root, self-conscious finally and paler than before, some guilty terror in her eyes, something beaten like Eddie Muller.

Alicia felt remorse, contempt, fear, and a big urge to run. She got to her feet and picked up her jacket and sneakers but then just stood there, unable to speak.

"I ain't a lezzie if that's what you're thinkin'." Charlene sat hunched over, hugging her knees and rocking slightly.

"No man, you just—" *You don't know how to touch without hurting.* Alicia couldn't say it. "Just keep your hands off me like I told you," she said, hoping that would end it. But she suddenly felt threatened, very far from home base. She wondered what time it was. A steady breeze was blowing and the air seemed full of salt. Above them the tops of the trees were all slanted in one direction. She walked a little way around the pond, watching the ducks. Water rolled off their bills. It looked delicious. "I think I'll get a drink," she said. "I'm awfully thirsty."

"You don't want this water," Charlene said, getting up. "People throw all kind of things in the pond. C'mon, let's go."

Suppose she'd come here alone and had drunk it? Alicia saw herself dead in the pond with the ducks swimming over her head. She decided that despite everything weird about Charlene she'd better stick with her, or she might not make it to Shore Farms alive.

twelve

The shopping center appeared all at once, mirage-like, when they got to the top of a long low hill. It lay on the land like something spilled—Alicia thought of a pancake. She vaguely remembered seeing it out the bus window but she'd been too mad at Fay then to notice much.

It was still hot and muggy. While walking they'd heard thunder far away but though the clouds were dark gray and low now the rain held off. They hadn't found any drinking water either, despite several trips off the highway. Alicia was painfully thirsty, and she felt as if the wind had deposited a sticky salt film all over her body. And her hair seemed to be everywhere at once.

They stopped and leaned against the guardrail, looking downhill while a tractor-trailer lumbered past them. On the parking lot in front of the long

U-shaped Shore Farms building the cars moved and stopped, moved and stopped, their pace more like that of a city. Because of the dark sky most of the lights were on, and the place was crowded with more people than Alicia had seen since leaving home. A little one-building city, she thought, and felt comforted. She found herself wondering whether they had dollar movies in shopping centers. She thought she would like nothing better than to get a hot dog and a cold drink and sit in an air-conditioned movie, with her jacket around her shoulders and her knees against the seat in front, watching events that had nothing to do with her own life or Charlene's or that of anyone else she knew. But there was no movie marquee along the arcade that ran the length of the stores. Well, two dollars probably wouldn't have done it, she thought. Though she meant to eat, anyway. Maybe two dollars' worth would fill up the hole that began just below her parched throat.

"The last store at the far end's Bellemere Builders," Charlene said. She started walking again, silently. She'd barely said a word in the mile they'd come since leaving the pond. The dark circles under her eyes were almost as pronounced as Fay's. Watching her walk downhill now, with short steps that thrust her pinkie toes out of the holes in her sneakers, Alicia felt almost protective, despite having nearly fought with her. She seemed somehow out of place, even in her own environment.

"You're goin to see Mister, what's-his-name, Hatch?" Alicia asked. She didn't care but wanted to be friendly.

"I'm talkin' to him about dancin'." Charlene glanced at her, then hesitantly: "You want to ask him too?"

"I dunno," Alicia said, meaning *no*. "But I'll walk you."

The parking lot was huge. They had to cross a lot of asphalt before reaching the store Charlene had pointed out, at the far end of the building. A card taped to the door announced BELLEMERE BUILDERS, but the office was closed, a venetian blind behind the plate-glass window drawn tight.

Alicia looked from the closed blind to Charlene. "It's Saturday, you know," she said. "Maybe they're not—"

Charlene turned to her a face like a pale drawn mask. "C'mon," she said, hardly opening her mouth, "come with me."

"Say what?"

She grabbed Alicia's arm for an answer and pulled her around the corner.

"Help me get in and I'll give you some money,"

she whispered. "Then you can go to New York, right? I know where it is, all you have to—"

"Wait a minute," Alicia said. "I said I'd walk you here, I never said—"

"You said maybe you'd steal—"

"I was just talking, you shouldn't of—"

"Liar!"

Alicia froze. Something was out of control again. She twisted away. Charlene reached for her, whether to grab or push or what Alicia didn't stop to find out. She dashed around the corner and quickly joined the crowd under the arcade.

She walked clear to the other end of the line of stores before looking back. Charlene wasn't anywhere in sight. Alicia felt like a fool. Usually she had better instincts about people. I should have just plain listened to Gary, she thought. He said to steer clear of her, and he was right. She stopped and leaned against the last arcade post, watching the busy, purposeful people with their bags of shoes and shirts and groceries. They all seemed to be in a hurry. Every female person except herself was carrying something. Alicia felt doubly excluded—not only because she was a stranger but because it seemed that nothing she had to do could ever be as important as the errands those women were on.

She began to walk slowly back in the direction

she'd just come, past a pet store, a supermarket, a window full of lamps. Then she came to a beauty salon with a blue neon sign that said COSMIC CUTTERS. All the young people inside seemed to know each other and were in various stages of being washed, cut, and curled. From their grinning faces Alicia guessed there was a lot of joking going on. Maybe they're all high, she thought enviously.

She stopped and pretended to look at some hairstyle posters taped to the window so she could see herself. Although the details were lost in the faint reflection, she didn't like what she saw at all. One side of her hair stuck out much farther than the other. She tried to pat it down but kept missing the exact spot. Frustrated, she stared past a corner of one of the posters at a vacant chair close to the window, and at a sign that advertised wash cut and blow-dry for fifteen dollars.

If I had money I'd walk in there right now and get a haircut, she thought. *No you wouldn't, you'd take the four o'clock bus.* No, I'd— There were so many things you could do with money. She wished suddenly that the conditions had been right and she could have trusted Charlene. What else had kept her from stealing? Or was it that she wasn't used to taking money, only *things*?

Another chair in the hair salon became vacant. They probably wouldn't even know how to cut an Afro, Alicia thought. She turned to study the people walking by and didn't see any Afros at all, or anyone who looked Latin, and she felt as if part of the world were missing and she was its lone representative, a strange culture all in one body. She was reminded of the town in upstate New York where she'd gone to the Guild House camp, and she began to be on guard for expressions like she'd seen on Emily.

But no one paid any attention to her past their initial reaction. They seemed to see her and then their eyes slid away, and except for one or two men who looked at her tits they went on. No one made eye contact. She might as well not have been there. She walked on aimlessly, hoping her lack of purpose wouldn't show. If only she could find Gary. She thought of asking the way to the Y but was reluctant to get anywhere near a "general swim." And what type of person to ask, anyway? Her loneliness for even one familiar-looking face increased to the point of pain, and by the time she had gone halfway across the mall again she was as homesick as she was hungry.

But at least eating would be something to do. She stopped at an attractive restaurant, but ac-

cording to the menu on the window it was too
expensive. Then she came to a Woolworth's with a
lunch counter along one wall. It was empty except
for two women down at the end. Good, she could
hang around there for a while, in the air conditioning. She stepped carefully through the automatic
doors and sat down.

thirteen

It was a small ten-stool operation with one waitress, a young woman wearing extremely blue eye shadow. The two, older, women at the end of the counter looked like sisters. They were having coffee and cake.

On the wall a sunburst clock reigned over color pictures of hot dogs and ice cream sundaes, and Alicia had to count the rays of the sun to find out it was 2:25. It felt like midnight. Her legs were actually *tired*, she realized, like after a hard game. She tried to interest herself in the food pictures but they didn't look real enough. She wondered what had become of Charlene and looked out the window, but when a girl with blond hair came into view she turned away quickly. No more trouble. No thanks.

The waitress finished rinsing some glasses and then came toward Alicia's end of the counter. The sleeves of her uniform hung loose around her thin arms. Alicia's first impression had been of a skinny girl not much older than herself. But now as the waitress leaned against the counter Alicia noticed that the belly behind the ruffly apron stuck out a few inches. The girl was about six months pregnant. She stood inspecting a stub of pencil she had pulled out of her apron pocket.

"I'll have a grilled cheese and a Coke," Alicia said, unable to interest herself in anything else. She had wanted a hot dog but they looked too pink. Then she noticed that a tuna fish sandwich was cheaper. "No wait, make it tuna—on a roll."

The girl looked at her with eyes much duller than their bright-blue lids. "No rolls," she said, and bent to erase the *gr ch* she had written.

"Um, well, okay then whole wheat toast."

The girl shifted her weight and looked around at the bags of bread stacked beside the stove. "I only got cracked wheat and white," she said, stifling a yawn.

"Cracked wheat," Alicia said.

The girl wrote out the order, pressing down hard with her pencil, then moved slowly away as though she were tired, or dreaming. Alicia glanced from her face to her protruding belly and wondered what it would feel like to be pregnant and unable to move fast. She had always thought it might be nice to have a baby one day, just so she could play with it.

Then looking away from the waitress she caught one of the women at the counter staring at her hair. Embarrassed, the woman quickly glanced away. Alicia felt half ashamed and half angry. She tried to smooth back the part that kept falling in her face and make it stay behind her ears. But it wouldn't stay, it wanted to go up or out, not down. If I had another dollar I'd get an Afro-pik, she said to herself. Some fun to arrive at the Surfside with her hair standing on end, Fay would freak out.

On the other hand she had no desire to attract *too* much attention. Trouble and attracting attention to oneself were connected; she had known that a long time. She twirled herself halfway around on the stool to look at the store, which seemed like the city Woolworth's she knew only larger, and decided that after she ate she would buy a new elastic and at least try to shove her hair together. She felt different enough from these people anyway. It was amazing that one bus ride had brought her to such a different part of the country, almost as though it were *another* country, where she was a foreigner. Like Eduardo. How had *he* felt, she wondered.

She watched people moving around the store,

aware of the hum of voices. Yesterday it had been
the way people talked, the way she saw *them*, she
thought. Today it was the way they were looking
at *her*. Beginning with Emily. It was the hair, yes,
but there was also something else: the men in the
bar, for instance—that she was there at all,
seemed, to them, startling in itself. They re-
sponded more to the *sight* of her than to her behavior. True she was darker from all that sun. Was
it the combination of skin and hair then? Was that
all there was to prejudice—skin and hair? No—it
had to do with tits too in some way, it had to do
with sex. Alicia sighed, confused.

The sandwich arrived. Setting it down the waitress grimaced suddenly and caught her breath.
Alicia jumped back in alarm as the plate clattered
to the counter in front of her.

"Sorry," the girl said. "It's my feet, oh, they're so
swole." She bent to rub them and then with a sigh
straightened up. "But that's the price girls pay,
right?" She turned a toothy grin on the other two
women, who were, of course, looking.

They smiled back at her in complete accord.
One said: "Soak 'em in Epsom salts honey, soon's
you get home," and the other: "And cut down on
your salt, Mary Ann."

The waitress laughed. "Yeah, Dr. Martin told

me that," she said. "But Donny has a tin fit when I don't put salt in the food."

The younger of the two women shrugged. "Men don't want to know about things like that," she said, less as a complaint than as an indisputable statement.

Alicia drank half the Coke before she came up for air.

"Oh I tried it," the waitress declared, as though not wanting to appear a coward. "But he says it doesn't taste as good when you have to put the salt on later. He says his mother never left the salt out and she had *seven* kids." She shrugged and sat down on a chair behind the counter.

"Well what can you do," said the younger woman. Alicia, devouring her sandwich, imagined the woman had said those words a million times.

"Suffer I guess," said the older woman cheerfully. "It's all over in nine months anyway."

"But that's when you really start to suffer," said the younger. "You'll be running after that same kid on those same feet for the next twenty years."

All three of them burst out laughing. Alicia was stunned. She'd heard similar conversations before but this was the first time she sensed something inevitable, as though eventually she too would be swept into a way of life where pain and sacrifice were expected. And pregnancy and motherhood were just tits and ass continued, she thought. Everything about women seemed designed to slow them down.

She finished the rest of the sandwich and drained the Coke, longing for a piece of the lemon meringue pie under a scratched plastic dome on the counter. But a search of the wall told her nothing about the cost of pie and Alicia didn't want to ask the waitress. She always found it embarrassing to ask the price, especially of something probably under a dollar, and then be unable to afford it and have everyone know.

Mary Ann saw her looking and propelled herself off the chair. "Sumpin' else?" she asked.

"No thanks."

"One sixty then." She sighed, digging at the pad with her pencil nub. Then she put the check on the counter face down and fixed her eyes on a spot just over Alicia's head.

Alicia pulled the wrinkled bills out of her pocket. When the waitress returned with change, she slid ten cents under the plate and walked away quickly. A dime wasn't much of a tip for standing on swollen feet, and she didn't want to be anywhere in the vicinity of Mary Ann's disappointed expression when she found it.

There were only a few people at the back of the

store among the hair-care products. The saleswoman was absorbed in some tally sheets. "May I
help you," she said, as if she'd rather not.

"I'll just look around first," Alicia said. That was
what she always said to cashiers in the five-and-
ten. Seeing no Afro-piks, she took a long wide-
toothed comb off the pegboard display and
feigned an interest in it, though she couldn't have
bought it because it cost ninety-eight cents. The
saleswoman went back to her sheets. Alicia in-
spected herself quickly in the round swivel-mirror
on the counter. Her hair was not even close to a
combed-out approximation of wild; it was just an
allover mass of different-length corkscrews. Almost dreadlocks, like a reggae musician, she
thought. If she didn't comb it now it might get so
tangled she'd *have* to cut it, ready or not.

Worried, she went back to the pegboard. Still
holding the comb she found a package of three
hair elastics for twenty-nine cents, which she was
pleased to think she might actually be able to *buy*,
until she remembered she had only thirty cents,
and that twenty-nine plus tax would surely be
more than thirty. She thought briefly of running
back to get the dime she had left for the waitress.
But no, that was crazy.

God*damn*, she said to herself. She was holding one item in each hand, feeling furious and de-

prived, when a back door she had barely noticed burst open and a noisy group of kids filed into the store.

There had to have been twenty of them at least, calling to people they knew and laughing. They all had wet hair. The saleswoman went to the far end of the counter and began talking to them. Apparently one belonged to her. In the midst of this commotion Alicia shoved the comb and elastics into her pants pockets, under the jacket still tied on her waist. Then she walked to the back door, and slipped outside.

Her heart was doing the hustle, as José Luis might have said. She walked straight ahead, without looking back, away from the door, among parked cars in another large lot behind the building. The sky was almost black, the wind had increased, and there was a sharp sea smell in the air. Alicia felt cold enough to put on her jacket but didn't dare expose her bulging pockets.

She stopped behind a van to figure out where to go to get rid of the packages. The lot was full of people talking and looking at the sky or getting into their cars. The only other building in sight was a semicircle with a corrugated roof, which she at first mistook for an airplane hangar. Then she realized it was the swimming pool: above the double front doors, large gleaming bronze letters spelled YMCA. The doors were open.

A Y wasn't the place to ditch packages. But beside it was only a field with an old broken barn, and then trees. A shopping center wasn't at all like a city, Alicia realized. In the city after a block you ducked into a doorway to empty your pockets. Here there was nowhere to hide. And it was going to rain any second.

By this time she had crossed the lot and was fast approaching the open doors of the Y. Everyone she passed was going in the other direction. Several people glanced at her but she avoided looking at them directly and kept her eyes straight ahead. So fixed was her gaze that she almost walked into the familiar red scooter, which was resting on its stand in front of the building. She ducked between two cars, pulling at her jacket sleeves to tighten them over the comb, which had nearly worked itself out. The pulse in her throat was so strong she was almost choking. A long low rumble of thunder sent people scurrying and a man dashed to the door of the car on her right. She ran away quickly, straight out of the lot into the field along the side wall of the Y, expecting any moment to hear whistles at her back.

The weeds were knee-high and the ground an

uneven mixture of yellow clay, broken glass, and stones. She got to the end of the long windowless concrete wall and turned the corner. There was another set of double doors in back but they were shut. A few yards behind the building the woods began. Alicia plunged in and immediately got a scratch on her hand but kept going. She stopped only when she felt she was far enough in among the trees to be hidden.

She could hardly see. The plastic packages were impossible to puncture. She finally had to rip the cardboard with her teeth and felt like an animal tearing at something she'd caught. The elastics were the good large kind, smooth and thick, better than the one she'd lost. She rolled them onto her wrist, hurting the scratch, which had begun to bleed. She was trying to look at it in the dim light when another, louder and closer thunder roll shocked her into moving. Wind swayed the trees around her. She kicked the packages out of sight under some leaves, then pushed her way out of the woods and ran back to the front of the building.

The red scooter was still there. Only one door of the Y remained open. Suddenly lightning flashed and a huge clap of thunder rocked the air. A raindrop hit her arm, then another. She walked a few steps toward the open door, afraid to just run inside. Suppose Emily was there too? Probably she was! The drops turned into a sheet of water. She was getting drenched. All at once Gary shot out of the doorway right into her, and calling over his shoulder a startled "Excuse me!" dashed to the scooter and began wheeling it toward the door. Then he recognized her and his wet face exploded in a smile. "Open that other door, will you!" he yelled. "Just kick out the bottom catch!"

She did it. The door swung open. He wheeled in the scooter, then ran to secure the doors. Alicia finally had sense enough to turn around. They were in the lobby. The building seemed huge. Besides the two of them, there didn't appear to be anyone else in it.

fourteen

Gary was still grinning. "You're all wet again just like yesterday," he drawled. "Seems like every time I see you you're all wet."

Alicia looked down at herself. The T-shirt, soaked, was almost transparent. She might as well have been naked. Her nipples were hard again. Goddammit, she thought. She folded her arms across her chest and tried staring him down, because she didn't know what to say.

But he looked away from her eyes to her hand. "What'd you do?"

It was still bleeding. "Oh, I—got scratched."

"By a wild animal? C'mon, I'll fix that up for you and get you a towel." He came closer—very close but without touching—and put his arm on the wall behind her so that his bicep was in the vicinity of her nose. "Except I don't have any clothes for you today," he said, "because you might go tellin' everyone in Bellemere they were mine."

Alicia blushed and turned her eyes away.

But he was laughing. "You sure gave Emily a turn," he said, as though that were delightful.

"Well I'm sorry," Alicia mumbled. "She was just—" How to explain about Emily?

He left her and went to adjust the kickstand of the scooter. Today he wasn't interested in talking about Emily. "So what did you ever do with my clothes?" he asked, coming back to her.

Alicia frowned. "I brought them to the Bath House like you said. You didn't find them?"

"I haven't been there. I usually work Saturday mornings, but Charlie let me off today." He took her elbow and steered her toward a flight of stairs. He was unbelievably pleased to see her; it was just the right time. He felt he had really lucked out. She looked different: darker than the day before, her hair bushier, "like a Negro's," he thought, and risking a light touch, liked the unfamiliar sponginess. They passed under a skylight. Rain pounded it, hard as hail. He put a protective arm around her and she leaned against him briefly, like a tired child. "Those clothes must be real wet by now," he joked, trying to put her at ease because he sensed she wasn't.

"Oh no. I put them inside, right by your room—where we were yesterday."

"How'd you get in *there*?" He pulled her around so they faced each other.

Alicia shrugged and shot him a little half grin but didn't explain.

"You're lucky Charlie didn't get you on a trespass," he said with a laugh, and gave her arm a little squeeze before he released her and they walked on.

Alicia giggled nervously. Even if he wasn't a cop, anything to do with "patrol" was after all something legal. He wouldn't laugh if he knew what else Charlie could get her for. She shoved the comb deeper into her pocket.

Downstairs the air was thick with chlorine. Gary opened a closet and pulled out a large white towel. Very solemnly he draped it around her and stood looking at her with the corners still in his hands, as if deciding which way to finish the wrapping.

Then they were kissing. His tongue felt hard and tasted vaguely salty. He dropped the towel ends and reached for her breasts.

Alicia pulled away. The towel fell behind her and she turned, glad of the excuse.

"No, c'mere, *please*."

He caught hold of the jacket sleeves hanging

from her waist, then untied them and used the sleeves to pull her close before Alicia even knew what he was doing. He *was* fast. Charlene was right. He was also wearing soft sweat pants and he wasn't much taller than Alicia. Something was exactly in the right place. "Oooooh," she gasped without meaning to, then felt embarrassed and started to pull away.

But he grabbed her hand, and a stab of pain from the scratch brought her down to earth. "Let go, that hurts, man," she said in a cold voice.

"Well, you just let old Dr. Willis take care of it." In his exaggerated drawl she heard the self-important lifeguard of the day before and remembering Charlene's comments wondered, as she followed him past locker rooms and showers, whether he just calmly stuck it to every girl he liked who came to Bellemere. Probably, she thought. Charlene might be weird but she no doubt knew what was happening. She watched his shoulders as he moved in front of her. His muscles looked even better than the day before. Danny had muscles too. She decided she liked ugly men with muscles better than handsome ones without like Joe Viani.

They entered a room containing a glass-doored cabinet full of medical supplies, a sink, a chair, and a narrow iron cot. A window high on the wall gave out on the asphalt surface of the parking lot.

In the faint gray light it admitted, everything seemed blurred and touched with highlights of silver, as though it were a moonlit night instead of a rainy afternoon.

The cot worried Alicia.

Gary turned on a light over the sink and looked into her eyes as she held out her hand. "Don't look so scared," he said. "I'm not going to operate, I'm just going to put some peroxide on."

"That'll burn."

"Only for a minute and it's better than getting infected. That's a nasty scratch, how'd you do it? Were you climbing the jetty again?"

"A tree did it," Alicia said, then looked away with her face tight, waiting.

It stung.

She kept her lips pressed together to keep from yelling and managed to say, when he had finished and was searching the cabinet for something else: "Are you going to be a doctor?"

He glanced at her and smiled. "Yeah, I'm good at it, I know. It's that old Willis touch. My father wants me to be one. He's a druggist."

"It's a good idea—then he can fill your prescriptions."

"Yeah." He found the antibiotic cream he'd been looking for and began to smear it on the scratch. "But I'm not into medicine." It was a complaint.

He felt compelled to discuss his difficulties with her, he didn't ask himself why. "I'm into phys ed," he added, not wanting to seem lacking in ambition.

"Well so am I," Alicia said, watching as he put on a Band-Aid. "But a person has to earn a living."

"Why're you worried about earning a living? Some guy'll take care of you." He returned the cream to the cabinet and began washing his hands.

"You can't depend on that," Alicia said. "My mother has to work."

"What about your father?"

"He's not—there." But she didn't want to start in on that. She pulled the comb out of her pocket and looked in the mirror over the sink. Her hair was so tangled that she didn't know where to begin but began anyway at the side. The comb went in about an inch and then stopped.

Gary sat on the edge of the cot watching her, unable to think of an opening line. "How'd you get here?" he asked finally. "I mean, to Shore Farms."

"I walked." Alicia put the comb down.

"You *walked* here?"

"Oh, not by myself," she said, mindful of the "incident," then added slyly, to see his reaction: "I came with that girl—the Crouch kid. The one you told me about yesterday."

"You were hanging around with Lena Crouch?"

"Was I supposed to make friends with Emily?"

He didn't answer, and something about his frown obliged Alicia to defend Charlene. "Besides," she added, "Char—Lena's just a little weird because her grandmother gives her a hard time." She gave Gary her favorite defiant, come-on look. "Maybe I'm weird too," she said. "You never know, right?"

"You're not weird, you're beautiful." All at once he jumped up and turned off the light and put his arms around her. In the suddenly gray room Alicia felt herself become soft and shadowy too and leaned easily into him, against the sink. He smelled clean and faintly like chlorine. She let him kiss her, for a while.

The cot.

She broke away and stood with her back to him, watching endless rivulets of rain slide down the window. She had never before messed with someone she didn't know, someone to whom she couldn't say, *"Okay, stop now."* Though it was true she had stayed with Danny one whole cold March afternoon and let him do a lot, had even unzipped her pants for him to get his hand in. All without knowing him half as well as José Luis. But this one was a stranger and worse, he was older. He probably expected something. And the cot was just *there*, so convenient and comfortable-looking with its white sheet in the silent, damp building. Alicia was afraid to do anything for fear it might mean everything. And despite Emily wouldn't he try? After all, it was like Fay and the driver, she thought, suddenly upset at the terrible similarity. They were both here for a while and up for grabs.

That shook her.

"What's the matter?" he said. He came up behind her and slid his hand along her ribs and then under her breast.

"Oh I don't know," she said impatiently, pushing his hand down, but holding it and resting against his embrace. "I do and I don't, you know what I mean?" She turned in his arms and looked up at him.

He seemed puzzled.

"I mean—do you make out with every girl in Bellemere?" That was not what she meant, but it served.

He looked offended. "Look—I'm just . . . a guy," he said. "What gave you that idea?" He let go of her and with a sigh sat on the bed. "Boy am I tired," he said. "I hardly had any sleep." He yawned and stretched himself out full length, then lay watching her, thinking she looked like a picture he'd seen somewhere. He wondered again what she was. And where the hell had Lena dragged her to make her look so weary? "You look tired too," he said.

"Yeah, I am," Alicia admitted but didn't move.

"Then take a load off your feet, stupid," he said with affection, as if they knew each other well enough to say such things.

Alicia laughed. He was fast but he was easy, too. She *did* like him. She sat down cautiously on the edge of the cot. Neither of them spoke for a minute.

Then he asked: "Are you Puerto Rican?" as though the question had been on his mind for hours.

Here it comes. "Not exactly," she said. "My father's from the Dominican Republic."

"Oh." He didn't know or particularly care where it was, though he wanted to be able to think that he had been with her, believing as he did in the stereotype of the passionate Latin temperament.

The rain, changing direction, hammered at the window. In the lot a car motor started and then died. "You know you're really beautiful," he said quietly. He ran his hand across her hair, casually passing over her shoulder to her breast.

Alicia shivered, then grinned. He thinks he's slick, she thought. He's sneaky. "You keep fakin' me out," she said.

He tugged at her arm playfully, trying to pull her down beside him. "A good athlete rests when she's tired," he said. "Why don't you lie down? *Please?*"

The hillbilly *please* got to her. It was like *plays* and made him sound like a little kid. She turned and put her feet up but lay on her stomach so he couldn't touch her. It was a mistake she knew but suddenly she felt so comfortable nothing else mattered. She was exhausted, and felt herself drifting off.

Sensing this, he didn't bother her, but put his hands behind his head and gazed at the ceiling, half asleep himself. "You know I was thinking about Lena Crouch," he said after a while. "It's terrible how bad some kids have it. My father says any guy in Bellemere could be her father. And Miss Thelma, boy. . . . I've seen Lena come to school with bruises. . . ."

"You go to Greystone too?" Alicia asked, curious.

"Greystone! What are you talking about?"

She told him about the car full of kids and what had been said.

"Jeez—someone sure fooled you!" With a laugh he turned toward her. "Greystone's a mental hospital!"

"A mental hospital?"

"Yeah. She was there this year when she ran
away, but Charlie got her out after a while."

It began to dawn on Alicia that all those kids
might have thought her a lunatic.

"A girl she met there was up visitin' her," Gary
went on. "Nita saw them walkin' on the beach arm
in arm and then everyone started sayin' how the
Crouch kid is really gay and that's why she's so
crazy."

"That's stupid," Alicia said. "They might just be
friends. Girls in New York do that all the time."

He didn't look too convinced. "Anyway I always
try to be nice to Lena," he said. "Except she takes
it wrong. She thinks everybody wants to make out
with her all the time, and they don't. I mean, of
course they do a little, because she's not bad looking, in fact I think she's really pretty, except you
never know what to expect from her. . . ."

Probably she likes him, and he teases her,
Alicia thought. Probably she was jealous when I
talked about him. . . . She lay feeling sorry for
Charlene while feeling warm and drowsy herself
lying next to this comfortable person, who was
again stroking her shoulder with such tenderness.
How nice it was to be touched like this. It made
up for past injustice. It made up for Fay's drunken
display and Charlene's rough excesses. Alicia was

overcome with good feeling and wanted to turn to Gary and kiss him. But she also wanted to press herself against him and trusted herself even less than she trusted him. "Well poor Lena," she said instead, sitting up.

"Poor Lena—what about poor me? Look—look what you've done!" He took her hand and put it on his crotch, then closed his hand over hers.

Alicia pulled away. "That's not *my* fault," she whispered.

"Yes it is," he said seriously. "It's because of the way you move. Yesterday I got hard watchin' you climb that fence, the way you handle your legs. . . ."

Loving compliments, Alicia beamed.

"I'd love to see you dance," he said, and as if the idea were almost too much for him, he seized her and pulled her down.

"I bet you can scre-ewww too," he whispered. He planted his mouth on hers and shoved his hand inside her pants, so fast that in one split second his finger was there in the wet hair, rubbing.

"Oh no," Alicia said. She felt as though she'd gone through the ceiling.

"Oh come on, please," he breathed. "You know you want to as much as I do. Please."

Alicia's mind was a blur. All the edges of things were blurred in the silver light. He had her pants

down around her thighs, her shirt up to her arm-
pits. "No, wait," she whispered. "I don't want . . ."
But she did, and he was rubbing it on her, it was
going to go in—

Then a door upstairs slammed hard, and the
noise echoed toward them through the building.
Gary rolled off her and almost fell on the floor,
yanking up his pants, pulling at the drawstring.
"Oh my God, it's Weston already. Get up, hurry,"
he said. "*Get up.*"

Alicia lay stunned and trembling. She pulled
her pants over her hips and stood up to do the
zipper, her movements impossibly slow, like someone dreaming. Before she managed to fasten the
snap he had piled the jacket into her arms and was
pushing her out the door.

"Listen, there's stairs at the end of this corri-
dor," he whispered. "At the top are safety doors.
They're not locked. Push hard and you'll get out.
I'll see you later." He gave her a little shove and
then ran in the opposite direction.

Alicia started running. She felt sick and tasted
tuna fish sandwich, and she had to pee so bad that
each time her heart pounded she thought she was
going to piss in her pants, which were already wet
and sticky. At the top of the stairs she stopped,
hearing movement and people talking not far
away. She gave one of the doors he had mentioned

a push, but it didn't move. It had a crossbar like a school door. She pushed hard on that and the door swung open noisily. She fell out with it and found herself in front of the double doors she had seen earlier, facing the woods. She stopped to put her jacket on, for there was still a steady light rain. Then she ran around the corner.

fifteen

Alicia shifted uncomfortably on the cement curb at the side of the shopping center building. Her back was to the door where she'd left Charlene; two hundred feet in front of her the wet highway appeared and disappeared under a flashing yellow signal.

She had no idea what time it was but it had to be past five—although the sky was still light the woods on the other side of the highway were almost black. It was hard to tell whether Fay would care if she were late, maybe today she wanted to stretch it. With Fay you had to do a lot of guessing.

But it was the dark more than Fay that worried her. Walking the two miles back to Bellemere alone in the rain at night wasn't something she'd anticipated.

Alicia told herself again to get up, that she

couldn't just sit there. She had been trying to force herself to do this for the last five minutes. She felt damp all over and cold, and when she bent over she could smell her crotch. She could smell *him*. When she thought about that her gut contracted, but the pleasure signal was confused by pain. She had to pee so *bad*. If she didn't pee soon, she told herself, she would explode. She would be lying in pieces on the highway, surrounded by a puddle of piss, and Fay would be crying and terribly embarrassed.

And Gary would be overcome with guilt and throw himself under a car. Hah.

A gas station would do except there wasn't one. She would have to find a bathroom in a store, maybe the hair salon had one.

A gust of wind sent rain into her face. With a shiver Alicia stood up, buttoned her jacket, and walked around the corner under the arcade. She could see the bush of her hair even without looking: it had become part of her peripheral vision. It really did look like dreadlocks, she thought; maybe people would take her for a reggae musician. But probably they didn't know about reggae musicians in Bellemere. Or maybe they did from TV. Anyway this was what she was, with no alteration possible. Because the comb and elastics were lost. The elastics were on the sink and the comb on the floor; she remembered dropping it when he put his hand down her pants. God, how that had felt. But then in her mind she heard his voice again: "Get up." He might as well have said it to a dog.

Over the bright mall lights an invisible sky lurked; the rain, hard again, came from nowhere. The arcade was nearly deserted and only a few cars sat in the lot. In front of the hair salon, which was closed, some teenagers were leaning on posts or lounging against the wall. Blue smoke rolled into the rain. Alicia sniffed, wondering if it was grass. She would have liked to idle in closer, see what they did, what they said, all of them probably in that nasal south Jersey accent. She thought she recognized the red blouse of the girl driver, the one with the wild eyes, whom she had liked. She would ask for a ride to the Surfside.

But no, it was too risky, she decided. She couldn't go up to those kids having to pee this bad. She had no self-confidence. She stopped behind a long dripping line of supermarket carts. Someone like Emily would surely give her that look of fear and condescension. And from the guys there would be those weird reactions she had got in the bar. (*See the sexy Puerto Rican:* was that what it meant?) They would stare at her hair or worse they might talk or come close enough to smell her, and then on top of everything else there would be that knowing look people always gave those who smelled like they'd been sticking their fingers in. And they would of course connect her to Lena Crouch. (*Admit it, Alicia, there is no Charlene.*) She would be another of Lena's friends from Greystone.

"Well fuck that," Alicia said aloud. "I don't want anyone thinking I'm crazy, even if they're wrong."

She turned and retraced her steps to the back parking lot and then held her breath, her heart thundering, as someone emerged from the Y. It would be Gary with the comb and elastics. But it wasn't. "I'll see you later," he'd said. Fat chance, Alicia thought, suddenly close to tears. The person who had come out, a man with baggy pants, got into a car and drove away. She walked on, noting again the old ruined barn at the edge of the field. An outhouse, she thought, I'll go there.

Squinting against the rain she headed toward it. But though it had appeared close enough, as she struggled through the still furrowed field the barn seemed to get farther away, and her pace slower and more unfamiliar, as though she were newly crippled. She slogged along. Slowly the Y receded on her left, slowly her heart settled. Like a stone on the rock of her stomach it felt: both heavy,

everything heavy. And it seemed that by acknowl-
edging these weights she became—in the space of
an instant—defeated Mary Ann of the swollen feet
and fucked-over, overweight Fay. Just like Fay. *I
hate to talk about your mother but she sure got
class. She got popcorn titties and a rubber ass.* All
at once some great sorrow filled Alicia for her lost
speedy self, her trademark, her significance. She
burst into tears but kept walking, through mud
that was over her shoetops, her tears and snot mix-
ing with rain.

The barn door stood ajar, half off its hinges.
Alicia wiped her eyes and peered in. On a pile of
old hay in a corner a figure sprawled; a plastic
bag, full, was on the bare earth floor.

Charlene got up and ran to her. "What's the
matter?"

"I have to pee," Alicia said, sobbing.

"Well that ain't nothing to cry about, stupid.
Just go behind the barn."

Charlene yawned and ran her fingers through
her hair. She felt calmer and more relaxed, having
slept as well as eaten. With her own feelings in
control for the moment, she looked curiously at
Alicia: this was the second time she'd seen her cry.
Charlene had been raised to regard the open ex-

pression of feeling as vulgar. "I looked for you in the Woolworth's, but Mary Ann said you'd gone," she said.

"Yeah I went." And if she expects the rest of the story she's going to be disappointed, Alicia thought. She sat down gingerly on an overturned bucket. The barn was dim and full of spiderwebs, which she wasn't exactly comfortable with.

"What're you cryin' about now," Charlene said.

Alicia rubbed her eyes, trying to erase the evidence. "I'm not crying," she said, "I'm just—" She shrugged and let the sentence go. She had the strange sensation that she needed to go somewhere and sleep it off, like Fay after one of her binges. Anyway she didn't feel like dealing with Char—with Lena Crouch, she remembered. Or whoever it was. Especially after what Gary had said. . . .

Pissing had been such a relief that she felt physically normal and she knew she needed to get out of there as soon as possible. Except as she sat, head hanging, the smell from her crotch was so strong, it occurred to her that maybe he had come? Oh sweet Jesus, she prayed like Diana, will I have to tell Fay? Just let it be all over, a bad weekend but a *past* bad weekend. She began to wipe her muddy sneakers with a leaf. Her hand trembled.

"Well you sure *disappeared*," Charlene said, offering Alicia a package of cheese from the collection in her bag. "I asked Fern and Richie and Nita if they'd seen you—"

Alicia sat up, refusing the cheese, and forced herself to pay attention. "You asked . . . ?"

"The kids in the car."

"Oh."

"And Mrs. Richardson, she said she talked to you. . . . She remembered your hair."

Naturally, Alicia thought. Charlene's story sounded like one of Fay's detective novels. "Who's Mrs. Richardson?"

"She works in Woolworth's—near the back door. Mary Ann said you went toward the back—"

Holy shit they *all* know each other. Alicia began to feel that all of Bellemere had been watching her. She imagined Mrs. Richardson, followed by the whole town, invading the woods for the rest of the evidence, the torn packages under the leaves. She felt relieved that the comb and elastics were gone and began to worry only that Gary might try to return them.

Charlene was squinting at her. "Somethin' happened to you," she said.

"Nothing," Alicia said. She wished she had bothered to check the time. Maybe there was really plenty of daylight left. She was ashamed of her fear of the dark, which Fay always said she'd outgrow. Someday. She glanced at the piece of sky she could see through the doorway, hoping the rain would stop soon.

Charlene's mouth lifted in a little half-smile. "You were with Gary Willis, that's where you were," she said. "You were gettin' your rocks off with Gary Willis in the swimming pool at the Y."

Alicia, wary and in control now, shrugged off the statement as though it meant nothing to her. "I don't put my business in the street," she said.

"Yeah, Fern said Nita told her you wouldn't give his clothes to Emily this morning."

Alicia was silent.

"You didn't tell him anything about me and Charlie?" The tone was threatening.

"No," Alicia mumbled, that alone an acknowledgement of where she'd been.

Charlene grinned. "Emily says Gary does it real good," she said drowsily. "He's always trying to get me into the Bath House." She stretched. "I never let him but maybe I should."

"He just wants to be nice to you," Alicia said, partly because that was what she wanted to think.

Charlene sat up. "Bullcrap," she said. "That's what I told you about the guys in this town. They always blame everything that happens on women. You sure you didn't tell him—"

"I told you I didn't."

"Yeah, but everyone lies to me," Charlene said with no emotion. "Besides men make you tell things just to get your pussy wet."

Oh lordy sweet Jesus, Alicia said silently, re-remembering her (*why call it pussy*) wet under his finger. She shivered, wishing to be miraculously transported home and out of her damp clothes, away from thinking about sex, talking about sex. She wanted to be on the bus tomorrow with Fay, even hung-over Fay. She wanted to be in school on Monday playing volleyball.

"I gotta go," she said, then after another glance out the door at the deepening gray mist behind the shopping center: "Are you by any chance going back to Bellemere?" She tried to keep the anxiety out of her voice.

But she didn't succeed. Charlene, picking up on it, turned a malicious grin on her. "Nah," she said. "I think I'll just stay here for the night. You can probably get a ride. You're doin' all right for a summer girl." She lay down on the straw again and closed her eyes but kept smiling. She knew she could say yes anytime she wanted to.

Alicia took a step toward the door. Shreds of black cloud were running across the sky. The wild-eyed girl in the red blouse might still be there. Or someone would take her, even an older person in spite of her hair, maybe she could get a guy. . . .

She saw again Paulie's hard round belly and thick arm, his square-jawed profile: "I'll ride you down in half an hour." She couldn't do it. She felt too fucked up.

"Isn't your grandmother going to get on your case if you don't go home—call the county or something?" she said.

This plea especially didn't escape Charlene. "Fuck my grandmother," she said. "Fuck the county." She grabbed her crotch and wiggled on the straw, laughing. "Fuck her just like your mother. Like you and Gary too." She stopped, meeting Alicia's horrified gaze. "He didn't pop your cherry, did he?" she asked, in the kindest imaginable voice.

She's really stone crazy, Alicia thought, suddenly fearful because she had never met anyone so changeable. "I've got to go," she said, and went to the door.

But Charlene jumped up and grabbed her hand. "Ow, watch out!" Alicia yelled. She wrenched herself away. The Band-Aid was half off and the scratch hurt so much she was shaking.

"What happened?"

"Nothing."

Intimate with bruises Charlene felt ashamed.
"Wait. . . ." She went to her plastic bag and turned
it upside down on the pile of straw. Oranges rolled
out, candy bars, small packages of cake. "Here,
come on, have something before you go. I got a
lot." She sank her sharp little teeth into an orange
and spat out the skin, then spread her arm out to
include Alicia in the feast. "No one ever gives me
anything but shit," she said, "so I always take
whatever I please." She held out an orange to
Alicia. "Here," she said. "I ain't forgot you gave
me those fries."

Alicia made no move to take it. "Greystone's a
mental hospital," she said. "Why'd you say it was a
school?"

Charlene smiled a crooked, mean smile that revealed nothing. Like Miss Thelma. "You don't
have to be scared of me," she said. "I ain't one of
those maniacs that hurts people." She tossed the
orange in the air, caught it neatly, and then sat
down amid the food on the straw. "I was in Greystone because I tried to kill myself," she said after
a minute. "I just wanted everything to stop." She
was silent, then: "But that ain't got to do with you.
I like you, you're a good climber." She looked up,
her yellow eyes honest and direct.

Alicia felt stupid. And mistaken.

"Here, sit down," Charlene said. She moved

over to make room, then held out the orange
again. "Let's eat some," she said, "and then I'll
walk you back to Bellemere." She shivered. "I forgot my sweater and it feels like it's goin' to get
cold."

sixteen

"Why can't you just go inside?" Charlene asked.

"I don't feel like being in there by myself if she's not there."

Alicia was trying to climb the apple tree outside the Surfside in order to reach a stained-glass panel that Charlene had said looked directly into the bar. But the limbs were wet and she kept slipping. Also she was nervous: Bellemere seemed dead. Eddie's was closed, the bank sign dark. Only muted sounds came from the bar; the familiar pitch of Fay's voice wasn't among them. And except for the cars in the driveway Alicia could have sworn she was not on land. The high tide roared as though it would engulf them, and the Surfside itself, fog-shrouded and lighted with lanterns, looked more like a ship than a house.

"Here, let me." Charlene pulled at her sleeve and almost yanked Alicia out of the tree.

She climbed down. "Don't let anyone see you," she whispered as Charlene started up.

"Oh no one can see in this weather, and don't tell me that shit, I know my way around here and you sure don't." She leered good-humoredly at Alicia. The dampness had exaggerated the waves in her stiff hair. She looked like one of the gargoyles on her grandmother's burned-down house.

Alicia still wasn't sure about her. In fact she had felt trapped with Charlene on the way back, when Fern's car passed them. She knew nothing of these people, or who was right. And then after an hour on the slippery highway she had tired of Charlene's complaints about being caught in the middle and forced to stand for something you weren't, and not knowing what you were supposed to be. Alicia herself didn't feel *caught*. She *was* the middle. That was the way things were, and she would go on from there: it was useless to think about only *that*. After a while she just stopped listening and began to concentrate on getting Fay and going back to the house.

Somewhere along the way she realized she had forgotten to look up the Sunday bus schedule. Fay would surely not know, she thought now, standing among the sopping, rank petals at the roots of the apple tree. She wondered if it was still in the

wastebasket and if she should try to find it. The
side door was shut.

Charlene, squinting through a bright yellow
panel, had begun to whisper: "McBride, Mr.
Cooley, Dr. Fairchild, Paulie White—"

"Just tell me if my mother's there or Will Taggart."

"No, I don't see 'em." She peered down the
drive. "I don't see his car here neither."

Alicia's knees gave way. But they're probably
at the house, she remembered, and the feeling
subsided. Of course, that's why Fay kept the key.
They got drunk and then went to the house to
screw and the driver didn't have to be home at five
because he was supposed to be making the four
o'clock run. Well, that was simple. She beckoned
Charlene down.

The rain had stopped. They climbed to the falls
to get a drink, and then sat resting. In the woods a
gray darkness hung, half moisture half night, and
the evening air was chilly. Alicia's feet were freezing. She rubbed them, thinking of Mary Ann, and
wondered, possibly for the tenth time since leaving the barn, whether Gary had come and if you
could get pregnant just from having it rubbed on
you. She remembered having heard about something like that, a girl getting pregnant in a swim-

ming pool in Australia. She would have liked to ask someone but not Charlene. Although if she waited until school on Monday, it might be too late. Too late for what she didn't know, but maybe it would be best just to give up and ask Fay. She grinned into the darkness thinking how Fay would freak out. No, she wouldn't tell Fay. Fay wasn't ready.

"You gonna just sit around out here and wait for your mother?" Charlene spoke in a low voice, without taking her eyes off the lighted windows at the back of the Surfside.

"She probably went back to the house after I didn't show."

"You sure?"

Alicia didn't answer. What was she supposed to say— "No, I'm not sure, maybe she went to an orgy with Will Taggart"? Instead she got up and leaned over to touch her toes.

"Well, I'll walk you up there anyways," Charlene said.

"I thought you came back for your sweater."

"It's in the Fun House, I left it there yesterday." She got up and started toward the driveway. Alicia ran after her, grateful for the company.

On Azalea Place every tree, every hulk of a bush in the weedy yards, was still dripping—*tic tic tic*

—all around them in the darkness. But now the
wind had changed and cut at their backs, and the
clouds were streaming ahead of them, leaving
patches of royal blue sky. Alicia put her arm
through Charlene's, as she had on the highway,
because it seemed easier and more comfortable to
walk like that, to be guided along an unfamiliar
street. She thought angrily of what Gary had told
her, about the girl from Greystone and Charlene
walking arm-in-arm on the beach, and wondered
what else Bellemere didn't allow. Certainly they
don't hesitate to fuck you, she thought.

Charlene began to sing, a tune about lost love.
She sang in a clear, sad voice with a little catch to
it. The song exactly matched the scene somehow.

"Hey man that's nice," Alicia said, meaning it.
"You're pretty good. Maybe if you can't dance,
you could be a singer."

"It's just country," Charlene said. Then she
chuckled. "My grandmother hates country. She
wouldn't even have it on the jukebox until Mc-
Bride just went ahead and got the records put on
anyway." Charlene was silent a moment, shaking
her head. "But I'm done with her now," she said
quietly. "I'm done with her and Charlie and that
dead whore of a mother of mine too. I'm done
with Bellemere. I'm gone."

"You're splitting for good, you mean?" They were already on the path, the gravel crunching underfoot.

Suddenly Charlene stopped walking and tightened her hold on Alicia's arm to stop her too. Something was happening at the Fun House: first voices, then the rumble of a generator. Then slowly, as though catching fire, the neon lights of the sign went on one after another, until the entire face of the clown looked down at them, its grin flashing bright red and green.

Then abruptly the whole thing went out. Alicia, who had stopped breathing, breathed.

Charlene's face was dead white. "Fuck are they doin'," she muttered.

"What?"

"Nothin'. I was just surprised they were still there. Must be past seven by now."

At the mention of time Alicia's mind automatically went to Fay. She hoped they weren't still in bed. Joe would always give her such dirty looks if she arrived in the middle.

They continued walking. The sign went on and off several more times, casting eerie colored shadows over the path. Charlene seemed nervous: she kept twisting and untwisting the frayed cord of her bag.

At 271 there was no car in front of the house. The door was locked. Alicia banged on it a few times, then just stood there, fighting panic—until her anger arrived, flaming, and the rational Alicia said: *Terrific. I knew it would happen. She just took off and went to fuck, the fat bitch, and left me in a weird hick town. With weirdos in it.* She looked at Charlene, who was sitting in the porch chair with her feet on the rail, staring at the Fun House sign.

She turned to Alicia a face full of sympathy. "You want to get in?"

Alicia frowned and sat down on the arm of the chair. "I don't want to break in or nothin' though. I told you, it's her boss's house, and I'm not about to get her fired. The bitch just got *hired.*" She felt better after cursing Fay out loud.

"Don't worry about it," Charlene said. "I know this house pretty well. I watched TV here all last fall before Charlie caught me."

Alicia followed her around to the side of the house. Charlene crawled under the porch and dragged out a cinder block, which she kicked through the grass until it was under the bathroom window. Then she climbed onto it and, just by pressing the window frame in certain places, removed the screen, which she handed to a very impressed Alicia. Then she raised the half-open window wider and put a leg in but changed her mind.

"It's your house," she said, grinning, and jumped down.

Alicia wasn't tall enough to get her leg up.

"I'll give you a boost." Charlene offered her locked hands.

Alicia hesitated, then stepped into them cautiously; tired, she felt heavy again. But Charlene held her weight and with no trouble at all she was soon astride the sill. Then her foot found the toilet. She swung herself over, and for a moment felt as accomplished as she had felt climbing into the Bath House.

It was much darker inside. Alicia walked stealthily down the hall, for some reason not quite sure she wouldn't find Fay and the driver sacked out, too drunk to wake up to ordinary noise. Or was she hoping? But nothing had been moved, the bed not made, everything was the same as they'd left it. She opened the front door to let Charlene in. Then she went into the bedroom and collapsed on the disorderly heap of blankets. She was so tired she ached everywhere.

Charlene sat down next to her, tense as a dog expecting to be chased. "I don't want to get caught here so I'm gone," she said.

"Wait." Alicia grabbed her arm, held it. And felt as she made the gesture some of the same desperation Charlene might herself feel. She swallowed, loosened her grip, tried to relax. But she wasn't about to stay at the end of Azalea Place alone; it was too creepy, too full of shadows. She sat up. "They might not come back till late. After you get your sweater which way're you goin'?"

"That's my business." Charlene pulled her arm free and stood up.

"Okay." Alicia didn't know what it was all about but she forced herself off the bed. "Then just walk me back to Main Street—"

"Oh you city girls are always scared in the country." Charlene leered at her, so pleased to condescend. "And by the way how old are you anyway?"

Alicia hesitated. "I told you," she said.

"And I figured you were lyin'."

She shrugged.

"You're no more'n thirteen."

Alicia nodded at the clear eyes that kept their yellow even in the dark.

"You see, I'm smarter than people usually think —I got some Crouch and Rittenhouse in me too." Charlene glanced away, lost in thought for a moment, then turned to Alicia with the same chal-

lenging look she had offered that morning in the
gazebo.

"Actually you could help me," she said. "If you
can shut your mouth and keep up." She stared
hard at Alicia. "After I get my sweater from the
Fun House I'm goin' back to Shore Farms and
from there I'm hitchin' to Asbury. You want to
come?"

Where was Asbury? *What* was Asbury? Alicia
sat down on the bed again.

"You don't have to stay," Charlene said. "You
can hitch from there to New York easy. I've done
it."

Alicia bent to retie her sneakers, stalling. Fay
would be back sooner or later. But when. And
what was she supposed to do in the meantime?
She pulled at the laces, remembering the way she
had hung her head the night before, trying to figure out then what to do if Fay's shit went on a
long time. Oh Ma, she thought, and somewhere
inside her the words were a sob, but then the
guardian Alicia added, in her accustomed, hard
way: *fuck Fay, goddammit, she might well be
anywhere by this time. Orgies, shit, let me go
home.* Her mind climbed into a car that sped
through the tunnel, and then on a fast subway
train to the yard, to Diana (help Diana my hair

my hair), to Danny, on the corner, in the
shadows. . . .

"I'm in a hurry," Charlene said, with a glance
outside. "Yes or no."

I won't do anything stupid, Alicia said to herself as she stood up. Aloud she said: "Just let me
get my stuff."

Charlene nodded, unsmiling, businesslike. "You
know the path?"

"To the Fun House?"

"Yeah. I'll meet you on that." She turned and
was gone, as if she had dematerialized. The silence
that followed was intolerable. Alicia saw strange
shapes in the corners and was afraid to turn on the
light to reveal them further. But she managed to
find the paper shopping bag from Fay's Scotch
and put in it her hairbrush, housekeys, and a clean
T-shirt. Then she hunted frantically for her barrette among Fay's curlers strewn on the dresser.
Goddamn you Fay, she thought, where the fuck
are you, how could any mother drag her kid
this far from home and then leave her alone. And
in the dark. Fucking bitch, fucking bitch. Fay is
why I get in trouble, she thought. It's not my
fault, it's never my fault. I'm *right*.

After that outburst she felt aggressive, un-
daunted, brave, and when she finally found the

barrette she shoved all the curlers onto the floor. No I am *not* like you Fay.

And then, having retaliated, she relented. She tore off a corner of the shopping bag and went in search of the pencil she had seen in the kitchen. The note she wrote said: Dear Ma, Went Home, Love Alicia. She stuck it in the frame of the bedroom mirror.

seventeen

As Alicia came out on the porch the wind scraped some bushes against the side of the house and she froze, frightened by the sound and the movement. A bright half-moon had risen. The bushes were gray in the moonlight and the gravel on the path was a luminous purple and gray. She thought of the gray light in the basement of the Y and then about Gary again, how that had felt, pressing against him on the narrow cot. She shivered, feeling excited now too—adventure like sex so quickly enraptured her, she loved the stress, the pounding heart, she felt light as air. Fuck you Gary, goodbye, she thought, very pleased.

She had the doorknob in her hand and was pulling the door shut when she realized she would have to leave it unlocked. Though Lennie hadn't much to steal—even the TV was small and kind of old. And Fay's clothes weren't worth much either.

Besides, fuck Fay's clothes. Alicia shut the door firmly behind her and crossed the street.

Charlene was all but invisible beside the path. The Fun House seemed huge, a sharp outline against the sky. "You get in through the back?" Alicia asked.

As if it had heard her, the neon sign flashed once and went off. Alicia's heart dropped, then jumped to her throat and stuck there.

"Scary, ain't it? Wait till you see how scary it is inside." Charlene giggled.

"Won't the men hear us?"

"Nah, we can get in through the storeroom. I do it all the time." She draped a reassuring arm across Alicia's shoulders. "And they'll be gone soon I reckon, then I can show you around. But you got to do exactly what I say now, hear?"

Alicia had never agreed unconditionally to do what anyone said, not even Fay as soon as she could think for herself. With Millie and José Luis there had been no bosses, they went together. She murmured something that wasn't exactly an assent.

"Yes or no?" Charlene hissed. "Say it right out, because otherwise—"

"Yes." Defeated, but there was nothing else she could say, having come this far. And Charlene had to know about the place—you didn't sneak into buildings at night unless you knew where to go. When Charlene started walking Alicia scurried after her like a puppy.

At the end of the path Charlene dropped to her knees and then immediately disappeared into the black space between the sand and the complicated struts of the boardwalk.

Alicia began to have second and third thoughts about doing this. She looked back. Above the line of houses they had passed was a soft, blue-black sky, high and wide and beautiful with one star. She wanted to stay and look at it forever. She wished on the star to become someone else, to be not herself—not Alicia Prince out trying to get to the yard but a peaceful person in a regular place. *Nothing nothing no one no one* were the strange words that passed through her mind. What could they possibly describe? She didn't know. She felt invisible. A sharp *psssst* came from below. Alicia took a deep breath, knelt, and then descended feet first into the darkness.

She couldn't see a thing at the bottom but was aware of coarse grass, sand, and stones and Charlene, who took her arm. As they inched along, she was able to make out the dark motion of the sea on the beach, close to the boardwalk.

Then they stopped at the doorway behind

which Charlene had been hidden the previous morning. Alicia wondered uneasily what she had been doing then but that concern became ir- relevant to the black doorway gaping at them now. She edged close to Charlene, who squeezed her arm and whispered, "Stay here."

Then she was gone, although Alicia could sense she was somewhere close by and then heard a squeaking noise as if something were being opened or shut. All at once a faint blue light went on under the stairs.

"Nobody but me knows this wiring's con- nected," Charlene whispered.

Alicia peered up. The stairs disappeared after the first landing. "Where's the rest of it," she said.

"Shh." Charlene came close to her and spoke right into her ear. "There's a door to the storeroom up there. See? It's a little bit open. I'll give you a boost, like I did when you went in the window."

Alicia stared up. The door she was to get through seemed out of reach even with a boost. "Why can't you go first?" she asked.

"Can you hold me up?"

She sighed. *No.* She began to see that although Charlene was the boss it was she, Alicia, who was making the enterprise possible.

They crept up the rickety lower stairway. Charlene braced herself against the wall beside the top step and held out her locked fingers for Alicia's foot. "What about you?" Alicia said, hesitating. "How the hell do you ever do this by yourself?"

"There's a rope tied on the inside door handle. Throw it down to me when you get up there. I usually leave it down but yesterday I had to get out in a hurry because of Roland."

It wasn't easy. Using the broken remains of the stairs and parts of the banister for handholds, Alicia managed to hoist herself onto the floor of the storage room. But as she fell in, the shopping bag caught underneath her and the hairbrush poked her left breast painfully. I'm too big to do this, she thought. It wasn't a thought to have when you were in the middle of doing it.

The place stank of mildew and was dusty. Alicia sat up, pinching her nose to keep back a sneeze with one hand and with the other trying to brush off her shirt, which she knew had to be dirty though she couldn't see it. Then she found the rope behind the door and kicked it to Charlene, who looked like a ghost in the vague blue light.

"Brace the door," the ghost whispered.

Alicia nodded, then wedged herself between the door and the frame. Charlene began climbing, swaying from side to side in the stairwell. The door threatened to shut on Alicia, but she held it

back with all her strength, and when Charlene finally flopped inside she collapsed again too.

Then the voices began overhead. To Alicia it
sounded like they were speaking another language, because the words were indistinct. But it
was clear they were having an argument.

"It's Hatch and that carpenter Roland," Charlene said.

One of them began descending some stairs,
heavily, and wasn't in too much of a hurry. He
paused several times to say a few more words to
the person he'd left, and each time his voice got
louder and clearer until he was standing just outside the storage room, shouting: "I don't care *how*
many hours overtime it takes."

"That's Hatch," Charlene whispered.

Alicia didn't care. He was just too close.

Roland called down again.

"Just get it done," bellowed Hatch. "You'll be
paid." He thumped past the storage room, a door
slammed, and then the boardwalk rattled as he
walked away.

"That leaves Roland," Charlene whispered. "I
wonder how long he's gonna be."

"Sounds to me like he's supposed to stay here,"
Alicia said.

"Nah, Hatch is always hollerin' like that. Listen,
he's comin' downstairs now. Shh."

They waited until Roland had left the building. Then Charlene led Alicia around the boxes and other objects piled in the storeroom and opened a door.

The naked light bulbs in the low-ceilinged hall they entered were so bright after the darkness that Alicia had to shade her eyes. The bulbs were reflected again and again in a long series of framed posters and photographs covering the walls. She went to look. The photographs were of Bellemere's every incarnation—from a sleepy town where a policeman escorted a lady with a parasol, to a bustling summer resort that had a much wider beach jammed with people, and a crowded boardwalk with little carts that sold ices for five cents. There was a picture too of a family. Charlene's grandfather probably, Alicia thought, because beside him was a younger Miss Thelma (her mouth tight even then), and with them a beautiful girl. Charlene's mother, Helene? To Alicia's surprise she looked like a young Fay.

The posters advertised special events at the Fun House in past years. There was a faded one from 1941. A woman in it was wearing a hairstyle that had just become popular again. "Hey look at that," Alicia said, stopping.

"Come on," Charlene said from the stairs at the end of the hall.

"But you said you'd show me around."

"Come on up here, you'll see more."

The stairs led to a silent red-carpeted lobby with four doors: red blue yellow green.

"Go ahead, open one," Charlene said, smirking.

Alicia hesitated, then went to the blue door and gave it a slight push.

It flew open. A ghostly laugh came from inside a narrow passage. She jumped back.

Charlene laughed. "Go 'head."

"Are you kidding? I wouldn't go in there for a hundred dollars." Alicia said. "What is it?"

"It's just a trick—the door closes behind you and you have to find your way out, except it's dark and you kinda get lost, but you do get out eventually. It's just all that weird laughin'. . . ."

"Well no thanks."

"Oh it's fine when you've got someone to hold," Charlene said. "Then you'll be screamin' and bumpin' up together." She giggled and came close to Alicia. "Like you and Gary," she said, and suddenly threw her arms around Alicia's neck and began gyrating, only her bumps and grinds weren't directed toward Alicia really, they could have been for anyone.

"Hey get off, what the fuck—" Alicia backed away into the center of the room. Charlene's head was thrown back and she was laughing.

"Don't you just get that feelin' sometimes?" she said. "Don't you just *get* it?"

Alicia understood her all right, but something about the attitude was all wrong; she felt wary again. "Let's hurry up and get out of here," she said in a low voice. "I don't want to see any more."

Charlene's eyes flashed. "Well my sweater's upstairs," she said.

They went up another, narrower, flight of stairs to an uncarpeted hall, off which opened a number of small rooms. Alicia followed Charlene into one of them, where a light was on, and the carpenter's supplies were strewn over a desk. "Look, I wanted to see the Fun House part, not offices," she said. "Let's go."

"Just hold your horses." Charlene turned suddenly and almost walked into Alicia, who jumped aside to avoid another violent embrace. But Charlene ran past her into the hall, muttering, "He must've moved that desk." She seemed to have forgotten Alicia. She poked her head into one room and then withdrew it and ran to the last in the row.

Alicia followed her inside. There was a high casement window on the wall to her left. It was wide open, propped at an angle with a pole. Moonlight streamed in, the sea crashed almost below them, the Bath House and even the Surfside seemed right next door. Alicia felt as if everyone in Bellemere could see her.

Charlene was opening the drawers of a desk. "Look in those cabinets on the wall," she said.

"For your sweater?" Cautiously Alicia opened one: neat stacks of paper, balloons in boxes, a coffee can, adding machine rolls. There was a top shelf though. "You think it could be up there?" she said, in a low voice because she felt so exposed.

"God*damn!*" Charlene said, slamming a drawer shut.

Alicia turned, frightened. "*Shh.*"

Charlene paid no attention. Maybe she hadn't heard. Alicia left the cabinet open and went to the desk. "What's the matter?" she whispered.

Charlene wouldn't answer. She kept opening and then slamming shut one drawer after another and then the same drawers again. There were papers on the desk and some of them fell on the floor. A small lamp fell over and the shade went rolling across the room.

Oh my God she's having a fit.

Alicia was saying this to herself when over the noise Charlene was making she heard the rattle of loose boards in the boardwalk, a man's heavy step. Then a door slammed somewhere downstairs. "Come on," she said as loud as she dared, grabbing Charlene's arm, "someone's here, they came back."

She went to the doorway. Charlene came out from behind the desk, holding something, Alicia thought, but in her fright couldn't have cared less.

"Just follow me," Charlene said, and her eyes were yellow and shining. She grabbed Alicia's arms and pulled her into the hall and then still holding her, squeezing, said, "Just *follow* me, hear? Just *follow* me. And thanks." Then she gave Alicia a quick kiss on the mouth and ran downstairs.

Stunned, Alicia hesitated, then realizing there was no place else to go, ran after her. But when she got to the carpeted lobby the yellow door was closing behind Charlene, and Roland the carpenter, an expression of shocked surprise on his face, had just appeared at the head of the stairs. Seeing Alicia his mouth opened, then a shout came from it. She made a dash for the nearest door, not the yellow across the room but the red one. It sprang open at her touch and then slammed shut.

eighteen

He didn't come after her. Alicia ran to the end of a mirrored hall, or what she thought was the end, and came up against herself. Only she was hard glass and distorted. She bounced off the glass and turned around. Another hallway led off the one she had come in. She ran through it to the end, watching herself grow larger as she approached, only this time the mirror at the end was distorted in specific places, namely tits and ass. She saw her wide-open mouth and terrified gaze as though they belonged to someone else, because below her neck hung huge melon breasts and where her normally slim hips and thighs were, a gross exaggerated swelling extended to the edge of the mirror. Even the small shopping bag over her arm stuck out obscenely.

The awful possible truth of this caricature in the midst of real trouble compounded her terror.

Little whimpering sounds came out of her throat. She turned and began timidly to retrace her steps. Where was Roland? He hadn't come after her and so maybe he hadn't seen her? But he had, he'd looked right into her eyes. Was he letting her go? She couldn't hear anything, no sound at all. She turned, saw still another hall leading in the opposite direction and went to that, trying not to look at the mostly bulbous distortions of herself on the way. But at the end of this hall the Alicia she found was tall and skinny as a toothpick, and above the thin body her hair spread out like a bush and all the features of her face were broad, like some ancient African ancestor-statue of Eduardo Despres. She pushed hard at this mirror, hoping it would open because of a beveled edge at one side. But nothing moved and she was afraid to push harder for fear of breaking the glass. She went back along the hall and came out into what she thought was the center and then went again to what she thought was the door she'd come in. Only with everything reflected in everything else she wasn't certain exactly which mirror that was. In fact she was so confused she was no longer sure where she had come in at all, or what she had seen first. She bit her lip and pushed at every likely looking mirror but all of them mocked her and none of them gave, not even the one she thought

was a true reflection. Were her tits that big? She
went closer. This time the look in her eyes, like
that of a frightened stranger about her own age,
brought forth a self-pity she had never examined
so directly. She let go the scream that had caught
in her throat and burst into tears.

The crying made her wilder. With every sob
and wail she ran to another mirror and banged on
it—seven years bad luck or no—until she had seen
enough of her tear-streaked cheeks and the O of
her howling mouth. She sank to the floor finally,
and buried her head on her knees.

Why had Roland not come after her? The ceiling was made of soundproof squares like the music
room at school. Was it possible he hadn't heard
her? Did he think she'd already got out? Charlene
had said about the blue door that you were supposed to come out eventually. Or was the yellow
door the only real way? Suppose Fay came back
and found her note and went to New York? Suppose they *never* came after her—how could she
live? Alicia saw herself dead and decomposing,
reflected a hundred times, a horrible sight when
they finally opened the Fun House—next week?
Or had he said two weeks? She began to cry again,
quietly like an exhausted but inconsolable baby,
hugging her knees and rocking back and forth.

She didn't know how long she sat this way or

when she finally stopped crying but presently she felt herself waking, as if from an exhausted sleep. Fluorescent lights at the tops of the mirrors began to flicker, and one went off and then on again. From a distance came metallic sounds as though someone were flipping a lot of switches. And then there were voices. Quite close to her she heard Roland. He was talking to someone else.

"I had just come back from gettin' my dinner, you know? Because Hatch is crazy fer gettin' his office fixed by Monday. I was workin' overtime, you know? And so I'm comin' up the stairs and this here *girl* come flyin' down—the one Charlie told me to watch for—that Crouch kid, you know?"

The other person didn't say anything.

"So she run in *there*," Roland went on, "and I figger she cain't get out because that switch is broke—it's one of the things I got to *fix*, you know? And so I phone Charlie but there's no answer—so then I just run out to get *you* because I seen you on Main Street. . . ."

At this point the door began to open, only a few feet from where Alicia was sitting, and she saw first the glow of the red carpet on the floor and then the legs of the person who was pushing it open. She was too tired and defeated to stand. She looked up slowly, expecting a flashlight in her eyes, but there was only this astonished face above a familiar shirt and dungarees, and she realized through the blur of renewed tears that she was looking at Gary.

After a long moment he said to Roland:

"That's not the Crouch kid, it's a girl from New York."

Alicia put her head down and dug her eyes into her pants.

"What were you doin' upstairs?" he said to her, shocked.

Unable to talk, Alicia just shook her head.

Gary turned to Roland, who was standing with his hands in his overall pockets staring at Alicia. "I guess you better go look upstairs," he said. "I'll wait here."

Roland muttered something under his breath, then clumped up the stairs. They heard him walk along the hall. Then a series of exclamations. He returned to the head of the stairs. "Hey Gary? Hatch's desk is all tore up—stuff on the floor and all."

"Is anything missing?"

"How should I know? It's Hatch's desk—you'll have to ask him," Roland said. His irritation at this delay was beginning to show. "Listen Gary," he said. "You take care of it. I got to finish this work tonight and drive way the hell to Kearney for lumber in the morning." He went back down the hall and almost immediately began hammering.

Gary stood in the doorway, uncomfortable and threatened by his involvement with Alicia. He had only meant to fool around, because she was so athletic and sexy and Puerto Rican. He should have known better, he thought now. He should have expected trouble. "Did you take anything?" he asked her.

Alicia took a deep breath and at last looked at him. "No I didn't," she said. "I swear I didn't."

"Then why'd you mess up the desk?"

"I—it wasn't—" She didn't know whether or not to tell him about Charlene. Had Charlene taken anything? "It was dark," Alicia muttered.

He frowned down at her. "But what were you *doing* in here anyway?" He sounded offended.

"I—just wanted to—see the Fun House," she said. "What the inside looked like."

"How'd you get in?"

"I—climbed. Through the basement." She tried to smile.

"Oh." That seemed to satisfy him, but he turned away from her impatiently. "Well I'll have to get Charlie to get hold of Hatch anyway," he said. "God*dammit*." He was thinking she'd messed up his date with Emily last night and now again.

"Can't you just—let me go home?" she said.

"My mother—" Alicia swallowed. "She'll be worried about me." She pushed herself slowly up the wall until she was standing and facing him.

He looked into her tearful eyes and was strangely moved, he didn't know why, then he remembered that she had been crying when he first saw her the day before. He was also embarrassingly aware that at the Y he had treated her, "well, like a whore" was the way he thought of it. But he wasn't losing his job over her either. In Bellemere you didn't just let people go even if you wanted to. The last guy had lost the job for exactly that reason. "Look I can't," he said in a low voice, afraid Roland would hear over his hammering. "You'll have to stay till Charlie gets Hatch."

"But my mother—" Alicia said, giving it one last try.

"You can call your mother from the station," he said, and reached for the CB radio on his hip.

Alicia shut her eyes and leaned her head against the wall. Now they would have to find Fay, and Fay would be drunk. Or they wouldn't find Fay until later. But sometime tonight there would be a drunk Fay to deal with. Why had she forgotten this? She wanted to die and be reborn with it all gone.

* * *

A few minutes later the boardwalk rattled under
the approaching patrol car. Alicia stood with Gary
at the entrance to the Fun House, looking out to
sea. The jetty was a dark mass that broke an even
horizon; the half-moon's reflection rolled with the
waves. It was a beautiful night, the kind you see in
the movies, she thought, where the boy shields the
girl from the wind. But Gary was not standing
close enough for any such purpose: he was doing
his best to pretend he didn't know her.

The car stopped in front of them and the tall
man in uniform unfolded himself from the front
seat. He was holding a hat in his hand. He set the
hat on his head and carefully shut the car door
behind him—not too hard. Alicia had the same
reactions to him as she'd had the day before—
dislike and mistrust.

But he was less frightening without his glasses,
although still too handsome in that way she didn't
like: arrogant over nothing. "Nice clear night," he
said to Gary, ignoring her. "A lot better than last
night, eh?" He was silent a moment, then he
looked down at Alicia. "Now, what's this?"

The way he said *this* made Alicia feel inani-
mate. She pressed a loose slat of the boardwalk
with her toe, just to prove she could still move.

"Roland found her," Gary said. "She said she got

in through the storeroom, and Hatch's desk is all messed up. I told you that on the radio."

"Uh-huh." He was studying Alicia now. "Oh yeah, she's that one came in yesterday on the eleven forty with her mother. I didn't recognize her at first under all that hair." He adjusted his hat and looked out to sea. "Well I called Hatch," he said, "and he sure was ticked to be interrupted, had some chippy. . . ." He stopped, cleared his throat. "He said there was a bank envelope with bills in the desk—petty cash for Roland's lumber, you know. Had about a hundred in it—in twenties—you find that?" He looked at Alicia's shopping bag. "You searched her?"

"No—uh—I was waitin' for you."

"Well, lemme have that then." Charlie held out his hand for the bag and Alicia gave it to him. He took it to the car and pawed through it in front of the headlights, then came back shaking his head and handed the bag back to her. "Call up to Roland and ask him to look—" Charlie hesitated, then said to Gary: "No—just go on up there yourself and let Roland do his work, you know how Hatch is—"

"Okay." Gary fled.

Did Charlene take the money? Had there been something in her hand? Alicia shivered. She put up her collar, shoved her hands in her pockets, and fixed her eyes on the Bath House just to have something in focus. Charlie looked at her but didn't say anything, and she began to feel, in addition to the physical cold, the chill of isolation. *Oh Millie, José Luis, where are you to press shoulders with? I'm going to have to tell on Charlene.*

The next moment Gary came running downstairs. There was a pinched, angry look on his face and it made him seem old. "Here," he said to Charlie without even a glance at Alicia.

Charlie took the envelope he was handed and squinted into it. Then he held it open to Alicia so she could see it was empty.

There was a moment of terrible silence.

"Well, miss," Charlie said.

Alicia looked at his handsome, solemn face. He was staring out to sea again. "I didn't take anything," she said. "I didn't."

"Well it's missing," Charlie said. "You'll have to explain that."

"It was Charlene," Alicia said, to her feet. She had never ratted on anyone before.

"What?"

"I mean Lena," Alicia said. "Lena Crouch must have taken it. She was with me."

Charlie frowned and looked over Alicia's head at Gary. "Did Roland—"

Gary went upstairs a second time. "Roland says he only saw *her*," he said when he came back down.

Charlie frowned. He didn't resemble Charlene at all, Alicia thought. "Well now that's right funny, little lady," he drawled. "I guess you'd better come on with me to the station. Gary, take a closer look up there and in the storeroom and all, and then call me at the station when you're done."

"Yes, sir," Gary said, relieved to be sent away from her. He turned to go.

"No, wait—" Alicia said. She wasn't going to let him get away. "*He* knows I was with Lena."

"Gary?"

Gary turned back and looked straight at Alicia without emotion: "I never saw you with Lena, you just *said* you were with her," he said, and then to Charlie: "This girl was over at the Y today but she was alone."

Charlie glanced at Alicia's stricken face and then looked back at Gary. There was obviously something he didn't know but he was a man accustomed to learning things slowly.

"Okay, Gary," he said. Then he closed a large hand around Alicia's arm. "This way, miss."

nineteen

It was a late-model car and very comfortable, with CB things on the dashboard. Charlie didn't say anything to her while they were riding. Alicia sat as close to the opposite door as she could, with the shopping bag between them. She glanced at him once as they rode past the brightly lit Surfside but his profile revealed nothing. His wavy hair looked blue-black under the streetlights; that and his high cheekbones reminded her of Danny Ting, the Chinese-Puerto Rican. It didn't seem as if he could be Charlene's father but she knew a lot of kids who didn't look like their parents. She hoped only that he would be easy on her. After all, she hadn't really *done* anything except break into their precious property and even that was an exaggeration: she hadn't *broken* anything at all.

Still she felt frightened and in the wrong. And when they found Charlene with the money she would be implicated. An aching horror began when she realized this. Could they accuse her of theft, in addition to trespassing? Could they send her to the New York court as a second offender?

A few streets past the Surfside Charlie swung the car into the driveway of an old three-story frame house, and then pulled up in front of a garage lit by an overhead floodlight with a cage around it. He shifted the car into park and gunned the motor a few times, lightly, listening. Then he shut off the ignition and turned to Alicia a pair of eyes that in the glare of the light were enough like Charlene's to make her rethink the whole thing. She stared back at him, suspecting there *was* a Charlene and a lot to the story she didn't know. Still he didn't say anything, but merely got out of the car and came around to open the door on the passenger side. Then he helped Alicia out and taking her arm not too gently, guided her into the house through a screen door at the back.

They went up a few stairs past a dark kitchen with dishes in the sink, and then along a hall into a large room—a dining room it looked like, there were cabinets full of dishes along one wall. But where the table might have been was a wide desk with a bright light hanging over it and behind it a swivel chair. On the desk were a phone and more CB apparatus.

When they arrived a red light was blinking and intermittent static came from the receiver. Charlie steered Alicia to a row of chairs along one wall and sat her down. Then, leaning over the desk, he picked up a headset with a mouthpiece attached. He didn't put it on but held it so the ear- and mouthpieces were sort of in the right place. "Okay, go ahead, this is C Belle Main," he said.

"C Belle Main, this is G Belle Beach," a voice said into the room. "Nothin' here, please advise." It was hard for Alicia to tell from the voice, but she thought it had to be Gary.

"Okay, come up but on your way check the BH thoroughly too. Got that?"

"Roger." The red light went off but then suddenly went back on. Charlie was putting the headset on the desk and had to pick it up again. "C Main C Main are you there?"

"I read you," Charlie said. "What else?"

"Okay if I go round to Em for five to tell her I'm working?"

A pool of loneliness welled in Alicia's gut, displacing every organ, bone, muscle. Of course he would go tell Emily, and the whole stupid little town would know, and eventually Lennie, and this would drive Fay crazy. She felt as if she were drowning.

Charlie grunted a reluctant assent and then laid the headset carefully on the desk. Then he made a sudden, quick turn and sat on the edge of the desk, leaning toward Alicia as though any moment he might leap. "Okay let's have it," he said curtly.

Bewildered, she stared at him. "But I—"

"Take off your shoes," he said.

She did, he looked inside, then gave them back. She put them on again. He didn't say anything but continued to watch her.

"Stand up," he said as she finished tying the laces.

She got to her feet slowly, hoping that her knees wouldn't shake. But they did. She tried to steady herself by pressing the backs of her legs against the chair.

"Empty your pockets," he said. "And bear in mind that you may have to undress."

Alicia was shocked. That had to be illegal; she would refuse.

"We have a matron on call for emergencies," he said as though mind reading. "All right, start on the pockets. Turn 'em all inside out. *Please*."

Alicia winced at the cruelty of his asking *please* when he was giving orders. She reached into her pants pockets and pulled out the insides. A small piece of lined paper fluttered to the floor—a corner of her assignment pad. She started to pick it up but with a wave of his hand he stopped her.

"Go on."

The two lower pockets of her jacket were empty. She turned them out. Then reaching into the left breast pocket she found—to her embarrassment because she had forgotten all about it—the English muffin. It was stuck. She tugged at it, tore a piece of the napkin, at last got it free.

He had his hand out. She gave the greasy package to him, feeling like a corny kid who had run away from home with supplies. He laid the napkin on the desk and unfolded it carefully, with two fingers, as if he were afraid of being contaminated. When he saw what it was he took a pencil from the desk and flipped the top half of the muffin on its back. Under the bright light the two halves of the muffin looked like a strange advertisement for bad food. He looked at them lying there for a few seconds, then refolded the napkin and asked for her bag. She handed it to him. He turned it upside down on the desk. Everything fell out in a heap beside the muffin and the last thing, which came out on top of her T-shirt, was the receipt from the liquor store that she hadn't noticed was still in the bag. He picked it up and read it out loud. "V. Rossi Wines and Liquors, 40 Spring Street, $8.57."

He looked at her with terrible, sorrowful patience. "Do I have to call the matron now?"

Alicia shrugged and sat down, shaking her head back and forth, back and forth, because that helped her self-control. "I didn't take it, I swear. Char—Lena must have."

Charlie began pacing the room. The humid weather had worn him down. At noon he had fallen asleep and then woke when the storm hit, feeling some vague worry that he had relaxed his vigilance about Bellemere.

And now he saw it was true. He came back to his desk, reached for the headset again, and fiddled with some of the dials on the receiver. "Come in G Belle Beach, G Belle Beach, this is C Belle Main."

He said it three more times before Gary answered. When he did he was laughing and there was music behind him.

To Alicia it was like hearing that other world, where people lived who never found themselves alone in police stations, where everyone was happy and cozy and loving like on TV, and had enough money to go from one place to the other if they wanted to. The sound of it made her feel worse.

"Gary?" Charlie leaned tiredly on one elbow and spoke into the headset. "Ride over to the Surfside and ask Miss Thelma to let you bring Lena on down here. Don't tell her what it's about, just ask her to come on down."

"Bring Lena down to the station?"

"That's what I said."

"Yessir." Even over the static Alicia could tell he was angry.

Charlie cut the connection and tossed the headset onto the desk. Then he got up and went into the kitchen and came back with two cans of soda. He gave one to Alicia, then opened the other and took a drink as he sat down. He was frowning. "And where exactly did you last see Lena?"

"In the Fun House," Alicia said. "She was going out the yellow door."

"And where was she going?"

"I don't—I think—" It was so hard to tell on people. "To Shore Farms," she said finally.

He waited. "To get a hitch to Asbury," she said.

That was what he wanted. "And you were going with her?"

"Well, yeah, I—" Alicia looked at him over the rim of the can and felt afraid again. He seemed so unfeeling.

"Yes? You were going to Shore Farms with Lena," he repeated. "To get a hitch to Asbury."

"Yes."

"And your mother?"

Alicia opened the soda and took a long drink. Maybe he knew more than he was letting on. "What about my mother," she said.

"How old are you, miss?" He leaned toward her across the desk.

"Thirteen."

"Um." He sat back. "Did your mother—" He was suddenly struck by her darkness and kinky hair in contrast to his memory of blond Fay. "That *was* your mother you came with yesterday?"

Alicia nodded, feeling the cold intrusion of *that* again.

"She knew you were leaving?"

"I left her a note."

"She's not on Azalea Place now?"

"No."

"Where is she?"

Alicia suddenly felt like laying some of it on Fay. "She was supposed to be in the Surfside but she wasn't so I thought she was at the house but she wasn't, so that's when I decided—" She stopped. Talking too much.

"What?"

"Huh?"

"Decided to what?"

"To go to New York. Home."

"I thought you were going to Asbury with Lena."

"She said I could get home from there."

The CB light went on at that moment, and Charlie reached for the headset but didn't take his eyes off Alicia.

Gary's voice came on, far away and indistinct. "C Belle Main, C Belle Main."

"Roger over."

"Miss Thelma says she's been gone since noon."

Charlie made a face. "Well, check the highway to Shore Farms and then come back here, okay?"

Gary's answer was drowned in static and then some loud country music burst out of the headset. Charlie threw it down and sat glowering at it. Alicia wanted to laugh, which would have been a relief, but she didn't dare.

Charlie passed a hand over his face before reaching into his desk for a form. "I think we'd better start from the beginning," he said.

"Are you—booking me?" This was really going to do it now, Alicia thought. And for nothing. Just like on West 81st. And what if they didn't find Charlene or the money?

"Name," Charlie said.

twenty

"And when did you first meet up with Lena?"

"This morning."

Charlie leaned back in his chair, watching her. A little dark nervous bird, he thought. He rocked back and forth a minute—making people wait pleased him. Then he asked, "And why were you running from my car around noontime?"

"Running?" Alicia's heart began to pound for no reason, exactly as it had then.

"You ran into the Surfside. Were you with Lena then?"

"No—well, yes, I had just been, and later—"

"Slow down, miss—Alicia, is it?" He looked at the paper full of statistics he had just collected. "A-li-ci-a. . . ." he labored over the syllables. "Is that how you say it? Prince?" He leaned back again. "How'd you get a name like Alicia Prince?"

"My grandfather changed it from Pryzynski."

He stared at her with a kind of blank curiosity, waiting for more.

"I'm a Polaminican," Alicia said, thinking maybe he'd let her go if she could amuse him.

His expression didn't change. "What is that?" he asked finally.

Alicia forced a smile, sincere-looking she hoped, and explained.

His eyes widened and he looked away in confusion once he understood her. It was a shock to him that a child could laugh at a situation he thought was a terrible burden. To him there was something vulgar and lewd about *miscegenation*, as he thought of it.

Alicia watched his frightened response as though she had spoken another language and been misinterpreted. She felt isolated and nervous, foreign. A foreigner like Eduardo again. *Rescue me Eduardo from this room and Charlene's father.* She took a sip of the soda. It was too sweet and already flat.

"And after you climbed in through the storeroom where did you go?" Charlie asked, when he had recovered. Shifting his weight forward abruptly, he made a loud noise with his chair, startling Alicia and putting her off-guard.

"Well I went to look at the pictures but Charlene—"

I HATE TO TALK ABOUT YOUR MOTHER 221

"Sharlie . . . ?" He picked it up right away. "You said you were with Lena."

Alicia froze behind the soda can. "I meant Lena," she said. Lamely.

He was still glaring at her, even more suspicious now (what, a *third* one?) when a doorbell rang at the front of the house. He got up and went out, locking the door behind him.

She heard him bring someone into the next room—probably the living room she thought. Then that shrill, imperious voice: "What did you want Lena for, Charles?"

Alicia shivered when she imagined Thelma Crouch's tight mouth opening on the words. Leaning on the cane, wearing that bag of a dress with a ragged sweater over her shoulders.

"Sorry to bother you Miss Thelma, but there's a hundred dollars gone from the Fun House." The new deference in his tone was remarkable. "Roland caught this girl who says she climbed in with Lena, and the girl—"

"Where is she?"

"Who?"

"The girl, Charles. Let me see her."

"Yes, ma'am." Alicia pictured him bowing when he said it. Arrogant Charlie.

She put the empty soda can underneath her chair as they started down the hall, and when they came in, she was gripping the sides of the seat with both hands to steady herself.

Still she wasn't prepared for Thelma Crouch. Nor the long narrow taffeta gown, still elegant though so old the black had rusted. And Thelma Crouch herself, her face rouged and powdered, the lines smoothed, pride and disdain replacing the angry frown. Against the thin, finely wrinkled skin of her neck a heavy gold chain glittered; a pince-nez hung from it. Not one hair of her bun was out of place.

Alicia was awestruck: this was a tyrant with style, a beautiful old lady who knew how to dress. And Charlie, in his same uniform, changed from dictator to chauffeur. Who was really in control here? Alicia's self-preserving mind dissolved in confusion. She couldn't assess the class distinctions among these strange adults. To her people were simply rich or poor and divided into ethnic groups; apart from exceptions like Fay the rich were light, and like the principal, gave orders that the poor, darker, janitor accepted. Now, staring at Charlie and Miss Thelma, servant and mistress, she suddenly saw—but did not understand—why Charlene's middle position might be as real as her own.

Then they both turned on her and began to speak at once: "Tell*Aretheyouthat*—"

The old lady prevailed. "Are you that one from Greystone?"

Shocked, Alicia opened her mouth to deny it, but Charlie cut her off: "Came from New York yesterday with her mother. One of Lennie Moss's secretaries. . . ."

"The blond woman is her mother? The hussy Will Taggart had at the bar today?"

It was the amazement in her voice and the way she said the word *hussy*. Alicia didn't really know what it meant but she sagged in her chair.

She was really in it now, and Fay was drunk and couldn't help her.

After that the motor scooter was almost a welcome sound. Thelma and Charlie both immediately turned away from her.

"I sent him up to Shore Farms," Charlie said. "See maybe if she—" The noise cut him off and he went outside as Gary roared up the driveway.

Miss Thelma stood motionless after Charlie left, resting on her cane, her lids half shut. Then the scooter cut off, and in the abrupt silence Alicia caught her breath.

The old woman glanced up indifferently, as if uncommitted to the room because there was no one else in it. Once more Alicia felt reduced to a thing, as she had with Charlie on the boardwalk. It occurred to her that there might not be any way

out of this place at all. Had Charlene made it?
Maybe the machinery would keep going and overcome her—and implicate Fay too. She imagined
certain death for them both, two unclaimed city
bodies in a hick town morgue: Fay white and fat
and naked and dead, and Alicia herself sprawled
beside, not shattered as she'd seen herself on the
highway or distorted like in the Fun House mirrors but abjectly, pitifully dead. Unjustly dead.
For going with a girl to get a sweater. *Did enter
premises unlawfully. . . .*

Gary stomped in behind Charlie and stood
scowling in front of the door. He hadn't expected
to see Miss Thelma, who had made him feel stupid
and uncomfortable before when he'd come looking
for Lena without a reason.

And her, the girl, Alicia. He had no idea what
she'd told Charlie and he was nervous because he
had her things in his scooter bag. Even hidden
outside they connected him to her. When Alicia
moved to look in his direction he shifted around
so that his whole body faced the other way.

She got the point, as she had before at the Fun
House: *Whatever you say to the contrary, I don't
even know you.* She looked away.

Charlie told Miss Thelma that the object of
their search had not been found on the highway.

But she wasn't satisfied. "You're quite sure,

Charles, that there isn't some grudge involved here? That this one hasn't hidden the money?" The cane rose toward Alicia, who shrank back. The old lady tapped her sneaker with it. "You've searched her?"

Charlie reddened. "I didn't want to bother you," he said, going behind his desk. He pointed at Alicia's tumbled possessions. "She says there's nothing else."

"Charles, you ought to know better than to trust one of *them*." She said it so softly Alicia wasn't sure she'd said it at all. But what happened next she knew would stay in her mind, would always be with her: the feeling of helpless rage as Thelma Crouch's bony hand closed on her shoulder, as she was led across the hall into a small cold shelf-lined room, full of documents, loose-leaf binders, rolls of tape.

"Undress."

"But I swear I don't have any money on me."

The cane rapped her shinbone hard enough to hurt. Alicia took off her jacket, then hesitated. The cane lifted. She unzipped her fly and with shaking hands pushed her pants down around her knees, then to her ankles. Then after a quick look at Miss Thelma, she pulled her underwear down too. The crotch stared up at her: yellow, encrusted, stained. *Oh Jesus, the smell.* She looked up, tears burning her eyelids, then pulled her T-shirt over her head and stood clutching it in front of her cold hard nipples.

"All right you may dress." Miss Thelma turned away, then back. "And stop sniveling, we don't mistreat people here."

Alicia wanted to kill her. How many times had Charlene wanted to kill her?

She was returned to the other room. Uncomfortably Charlie told her she could sit, and gave her back her shopping bag. Gary, sitting at one end of the row of chairs, stared at his shoes. Alicia sat down feeling as though she were still naked because they knew she had *been* naked. The feeling made looking at them unbearable; she put her head back and closed her eyes.

"I'll drive you over to the Surfside now and have a look around town," Charlie said to Miss Thelma. "Maybe find her mother—" He looked at Alicia. He was still considering the slip she had made, that name—*Sharlie*? He turned to Gary. "You'll stay."

"But—"

"You *wanted* this job, Gary. You have your keys?"

Reluctantly Gary moved to pull out his key ring, which caused him to have to include Alicia in his field of vision. Her face framed by the width

of hair was odd and beautiful, and when he saw
her behind the shapes of the keys he remembered
her body as she ran the day before, holding them
out to him, and the feel of her flesh under his
fingers that afternoon. And he knew he would
touch her again if he got the chance, if only to set
in motion something he liked, some dark secret
she represented to him. But he had never expected
his fondness for women to take him this far.
How can you still like someone on the other side
of the law, he thought. When Charlie and Miss
Thelma left he was again staring at his shoes.

twenty-one

Alicia heard the door click shut, the purr of the patrol car leaving. And then an awesome country quiet in which she could sense Gary's presence, almost feel the rhythm of his breathing. Their chairs were only a couple of yards apart.

She tried not to think of him but to concentrate on *next*, which would be Fay, or if they couldn't find her?

No, they would find Fay unconscious on the bed but fully clothed, her big tits extending the Mexican shawl (the bra in her pocketbook now). Along with the purple towel, Alicia remembered, and a giggle rose in the midst of the ghastly uncomfortable silence at the memory of Fay's shocked face upon seeing that towel.

She tittered.

He looked up in horror, assuming for no particular reason that she was laughing at *him*.

"What's so funny," he demanded in a choked voice, when she didn't stop.

"Nothing." She put her face in her hands.

"Well then, quit that."

She couldn't. He bounded out of his chair and grabbed her shoulders, as he had on the jetty. "Well stop being a pain in the ass," he said, shaking her. "You've been a swift pain in the ass to me ever since you got here."

Alicia pushed him away and jumped up.

"Don't you curse at me, man," she said. But the enormous sexual tension existed even as she stood there trying to stay angry. Despite herself she wanted his understanding. "Just because a person gets in trouble doesn't mean they've changed," she said.

He looked guilty.

"And you're a pain in the ass too," she added, sensing her advantage. "Any guy who acts like you did to me this afternoon—"

"Well, I'm sorry about that really. It was an accident—"

"But what do you think I—"

"Well, why did you go mess with Lena after I warned you . . . ?" He sat down on the edge of Charlie's desk, shaking his head, swinging his legs violently.

He looked so hurt—like Fay, as if Alicia had

done something deliberately to *spite* him—that she felt contrite. "Well, Char—Lena and I, we're a lot alike," she said. She waited a minute. When he didn't respond she went and stood in front of him, between his legs. It was a position she took without thinking, to face him squarely, though once there she realized she had walked right into it.

He stopped swinging his legs, looked into her eyes, then slid off the desk and pulled her close to him. "You're so beautiful," he said. "I always wanted to have a Latin lover." He said it with such mystery that Alicia wondered whether he was really talking about *her*. Or whether being half, she even qualified. . . .

She drew away, and picking up the headset pretended an interest in it, thinking of the bop's Italian Stallion T-shirt to which he'd prefixed a ½. In silver: ½ ITALIAN STALLION. She glanced at Gary: maybe she should wear a T-shirt that said ½ LATIN LOVER so guys would know.

That tickled her. She began to giggle again but when Gary looked at her with suspicion (maybe she *was* like Lena Crouch?) she went to him and put her arms around his neck. And because his stereotyping her had made her care less, she moved against him slowly and deliberately. Like how he thought a Latin Lover might act.

He was overwhelmed; his face turned red. "I have a present for you," he whispered.

"Oh no," Alicia said, thinking of Joe Viani.

"Wait, it's outside."

He fumbled but at last got himself out the double-locked door, which he left wide open. Cautiously Alicia went to the doorway. Had he meant her to leave, was that his present? But who could escape Bellemere, she wondered, thinking of Charlene. Was it a trick? Maybe, she thought, with a kind of cold suspicion, probably he had really gone out to call Emily. . . .

She took a few steps along the hall toward the kitchen, where she could hear a faucet dripping into a metal pot. Then a loud buzz burst from the room behind her. She ran back inside. The red light on the receiver was again blinking. Over the static came a series of sharp noises, like people calling, and then the faint but unmistakable wail of a fire engine. And she was hearing it twice, first on the chilly breeze that came down the hall and a split second later whining through the CB. Then Charlie's voice came on over all this, as if he were standing in front of her shouting, all his reserve gone. "G BELLE MAIN BELLE MAIN OVER!" A silent, staticky interval, then: "G BELLE MAIN! BELLE MAIN? DO YOU READ ME, G BELLE MAIN!"

Jesus, where *was* Gary? Alicia dashed out of the room and through the kitchen and almost fell down the three steps that led to the back door. He was on the grass outside, just turning a worried frown to her. In his hand the plastic comb gleamed in the moonlight.

"Something's on fire," he said slowly.

"The CB, the CB!" Alicia whispered. "Hurry up!"

He gaped. "The CB's burning?"

"No, calling." Alicia said. "Hurry up!"

"Oh *shit.*" He yanked open the screen door and stumbled inside, thrusting the comb and elastics at her as he passed.

It was like any fire: smoke and noise and confusion, silent worry behind handkerchiefs, fear.

There was already a crowd by the time they got there, filling the street from Eddie's to the mall.

No one seemed to hear the scooter over the roar of the surf and the grinding pumper-engine. Nor did they think anything about Charlie's screaming at Gary for bringing Alicia and taking so long. After all he was entitled to be frantic; like everyone else in town he had condemned the Surfside to slow decay. None of them believed it could go in front of their eyes. A rumor of arson was going around: the fire had started in the stairwell. There were still people at the top-story windows, where the firemen were just putting up a ladder.

Alicia sat in the backseat of the patrol car where Charlie had put her because he didn't know what else to do with her. The car was parked at the end of the mall, opposite the crowd. She searched the sea of faces, worried about Fay, but then saw with relief McBride and Paulie White in a group at the front. The bar had been evacuated at least; if Fay had been there she'd be with those people. Alicia looked for but didn't see Thelma Crouch, then figured she was probably one of the black-slickered shapes around the trucks.

They dragged another hose in through the side door. The fire seemed to be spreading to the back. Smoke and water poured out of what Alicia thought might be the bathroom window. The apple tree disappeared briefly. She watched the goings-on with a strange detachment, thinking of the burned mansion up on the cliff. Bad luck for Miss Thelma, she thought: this made two. She felt satisfied because the fire was more justice than she could have hoped for. She wondered again if Charlene had made it to Shore Farms and got a ride. She was sure now, thinking back on that

moment in the Fun House, that there had been
something in her hand. Probably the money. With
a hundred dollars you could easily get far away
fast. Well good-bye then Charlene. The point
now was how long would it take before she, Alicia,
got out of her own mess. It seemed as if Lena
Crouch had got off easy.

She slumped on the smooth vinyl upholstery
and thought of lying down. Fires burned and then
went out, she had seen a lot of them. She wondered again why Gary had brought her. After
Charlie's call he'd just freaked, undecided, then
had finally hauled her to the scooter; Alicia had
leaned ecstatically into his back as they sailed to
Main Street, half hoping to ride past Emily.

Emily wasn't there when they arrived but now
she was on the sidewalk in front of Eddie's. Eddie
was behind his counter making coffee. The crowd
swelled. Cars pulled up in the side streets. The
people trapped on the third floor were being
helped down the ladder. One was a fat man in a
raincoat; maybe that was Hatch. A woman came
after him, a big one like Fay.

Then suddenly a new sound diverted her from
this procession. It began as a series of small explo-
sions and then mushroomed into a continuous hollow roar. Alicia sat up. Flames were creeping

along the shed nearest the house, the one with the paint and sprays where they had hidden.

Quickly she rolled down the window. She had just stuck her head out, trying to see better, when something incandescent burst out the shed door and went twisting down the driveway. Alicia gasped and drew back. It was a person on fire. It was Charlene.

Everyone at once crowded the driveway. If it hadn't been for Gary and Charlie holding them back, Alicia thought, a hundred bodies might have overrun Lena Crouch.

She couldn't tell from their faces whether they wanted her alive or dead. The moon shone on the black slicker of the fireman who was giving her mouth-to-mouth resuscitation. Watching that weird kiss, Alicia felt sick. Despite the wind through the open window she was sweating and her stomach felt queasy. She forced herself to look away. It was when she turned, her eyes still wide with horror, that Fay appeared on the ladder. She was alone, clutching her pocketbook. Will Taggart, with Lily and the kids to think of as he told himself, had left her in the hallway and climbed to safety over the back sheds so no one would see him.

Fay looked almost exactly as Alicia had imagined, only she was vertical. But not for long. The laces of her espadrilles were untied, and she was swaying. She managed to get to the last rung of the ladder before she fell.

twenty-two

Only the young and resolutely curious remained on the mall after it was over, after the ambulance had gone and all the Surfside's guests had been relocated, and the hotel sat with its lanterns extinguished, a dark blank hulk, beached.

Hatch had his money back; they'd found it near the shed in a plastic bag. Bellemere was quiet. Emily was on the mall waiting for Gary, with Nita to keep her company. The others also had their reasons. They were watching Eddie's.

Gary sat sideways on a stool at the counter with his back to them. He couldn't stand being in there with Emily outside, but Charlie was making him wait. He only kept his cool by closing his eyes and feigning extreme fatigue.

In a front booth with Fay and Charlie, Alicia stirred the hot chocolate Eddie had made her. She hadn't asked for it. He had merely set it in front of her, and when she smiled gratefully his eyes had filled with tears. Although she had no idea what he was thinking, his tears brought on her own and she had a hard time stopping them. She felt very fucked up. Again and again she saw Charlene whirl down the driveway, as though propelled into flames by her own angry confusion.

And now it had finally come to drunk Fay, who she could see was hopeless.

"But I left a message for you," Fay was saying. "The bartender was going to call me."

"Well I didn't see you so I thought you were . . ." Alicia tried to make eye contact with her. "You know, at the house, with . . ." She glanced at Charlie.

He was wearing his sunglasses. She looked back at Fay.

"Well you were with that lifeguard," Fay said.

"Shut up, Ma."

Charlie's eyebrows went up. Gary didn't move but his ears turned red.

Fay let the steam from her coffee warm her face because the heat kept her mind from falling apart. She was really aware only that she had no consolation. And the story was so confusing. She still couldn't understand exactly what it was Alicia had done. If this cop would only come to the point so they could go home. If she could lie down and deal with it later. Not now—now the room was reeling. "Well what are the charges?" she said finally. She took a sip of coffee and risked a look at him. But she knew drunk Fay was never pretty. "Just tell me the charges," she repeated, looking away.

"Well, trespassin'," Charlie said.

There was a silence. He was about to add that usually kids caught sneaking into the summer places out of season were released with a warning in the custody of their parents. But looking at Fay's soft, slightly trembling mouth, he found the statement inappropriate. She seemed as much in need of custody as Alicia. He didn't want that responsibility to fall on himself or his Bellemere. He got to his feet and took his coffee cup to the counter, where he waved away Eddie's attempt to refill it. He knew everyone was waiting for him to make a decision and he realized he was keeping himself waiting too. He wanted to close up the town and go to bed and send these loose women, as he thought of them, back to New York where they belonged.

"We won't press charges so long as you leave in the morning." He looked from Fay to Alicia as he said it, giving her custody, making Fay Alicia's baby. Alicia hated him for recognizing this.

Fay was anxious to save face. "Well I want to

leave *now*," she said drunkenly. "This place isn't *safe*."

Alicia looked up, away from Fay to the blank ceiling, the still fan.

"I'll drive you back to Lennie's place for now." But reaching for his keys, Charlie remembered giving them to Gary, who had moved the car from the mall so the engines could pass. He stopped in mid-gesture and leaned his elbow on the counter. He had never cared about women although they were always attracted to him, and he had no particular desire to tuck these two in. However, he did have some sympathy for Gary's weakness.

"You know Eddie, I believe I'll have that coffee after all," Charlie drawled. "Miss Thelma might be needin' me soon's she gets back." He turned to the figure on the stool. "Maybe I'll just let *the lifeguard* here drive you-all home, long as he's got the keys in his pocket. He's always lookin' for a chance to drive the car."

On Azalea Place it was freezing but less windy and the sea seemed distant. They helped Fay onto the porch and waited while she dug through her bag for the key, which she insisted on doing herself. Alicia stared at Gary's shadow, too tired to think of anything to say, and a little hungry. He just stood there looking at her.

Fay found the key but couldn't work it into the lock. Gary took it from her and got the door open. She went straight into the bedroom and lay down without turning on a light.

"Well, good night," Alicia said, facing him in the doorway.

He didn't reply. He felt sure that if he had anything further to do with her, even to speak, he would lose not only his job but also Emily and his star position in Bellemere. Despite this he wanted to kiss her.

On impulse Alicia rolled one of the hair elastics, the red one, off her wrist, and put it into his hand. "Okay, *hasta luego*," she said.

A nervous half-smile lifted his mouth. He looked at the elastic a moment before he reached for her, and kissed her long and hard so he'd remember. Then he ran to the car.

Alicia switched on the hall light and collapsed in a chair. Her heart was pounding, her mind was blank, her stomach aching. She dumped the shopping bag onto the rug and found the grease-stained napkin.

She still had a piece of hard dry muffin in her hand when Fay woke her in the morning.

twenty-three

"You know I've never been told to leave any place in my life," Fay said.

Alicia didn't answer. She was tugging at the frayed cord that held open one of the shutters. It had got stuck on a nail outside.

"And if you're going to make trouble every time I get something going I just don't know—"

"That's not true," Alicia said.

"I know, but—"

"Well what did you *want* me to do—hang around and *watch* you?"

"Don't talk like that." Fay looked hurt. She turned and went into the bedroom.

Alicia concentrated on freeing the cord. Replays of the previous day began in her mind. To stop them she tried worrying about Fay or being angry with her. But Fay seemed okay, although Alicia guessed from her too bright eyes that she'd had a

drink. And after this exchange she packed the suitcase and put all the sheets back on the furniture
by herself, without saying anything else, which
made Alicia feel guilty and nervous.

The silence persisted. They got their stuff together; Fay locked up. Then they walked slowly,
because it was still early, along the gravel path.
The last thing Alicia noticed about 271 Azalea
Place was the cinder block still under the bathroom window.

The Fun House sign cast a slanted shadow the
width of the street. Passing through it, Alicia felt
cold. She shivered.

Fay glanced at her. "Did you break into some-
place yesterday?" she asked all of a sudden.

"I didn't break—" Alicia sighed.

"Well, just *tell* me, goddammit." Fay stopped
walking and sat down heavily on the suitcase,
which she had been carrying alone. She was also
carrying her anger and it was exhausting. She remembered nothing substantial, only that the cop
was involved and the lifeguard, and that they'd
been told to leave. She fished in her bag for a
tissue. "I'm listening," she said.

Alicia let two waves hit the shore before talking.
"I climbed into the Fun House with this girl. She
stole some money and they blamed it on me until
they—found her." She tried to squeeze her mind

shut on the movie of the fireman's black slicker, the locked mouths.

"You didn't steal anything?"

"No." *Not from there.*

"Then why were you hanging around with that girl?" Tears welled in Fay's eyes.

"Because—"

"What?"

"She was—stuck in the middle." Alicia began to cry as she said it.

"What are you *talking* about?" Fay gave her a helpless look, then stood up and took Alicia in her arms, yearning as Alicia had the day before, for that romantic "normal life" she could never expect. And there was more to it, she knew, something remained unsaid. It must have to do with a man, she thought. With a sigh she turned Alicia loose. "Did you, I mean, did that lifeguard, you know—"

"No." Alicia, rubbing her eyes, would not meet Fay's. There was no sense telling her now. Maybe later, after asking Diana.

Fay blew her nose and shouldered her pocketbook. Alicia always left a lot out. It occurred to her that Lennie might hear stories, but the idea was too threatening and she dismissed it. "You carry it now," she said, indicating the suitcase.

"How'd you find out what time the bus leaves?"
Alicia was glad to ask a simple question.

"I found a bus schedule in the Surfside yesterday, in the bathroom."

Alicia stared at the rutted asphalt as she
reached for the handle of the suitcase, daring yesterday's movie to start again. But it seemed finished. All they had to do now was get home.

When they got to Main Street the empty bus
was parked at the mall with its door open; there
was no sign of a driver. They got in anyway and
sat down, together, at the front. Fay was relieved
about that, as she had begun to feel light-headed
again.

Neither of them expected Charlie. A surge of
sick fear overtook Fay when the patrol car appeared. Alicia's heart sank too: what *now*.

Mounting the first step, Charlie beckoned her.
"One more question, please, miss."

"Yessir," Alicia whispered, goody-girl, her tone
begging his indulgence. She could feel Fay stiff as
a board beside her. She got up and walked to the
steps.

"That other name you mentioned yesterday—
Sharlie?"

"Charlene." She stepped back and clutched the
slick steel of the pole behind the driver's seat.

He remained silent. She looked up after a minute, only to find he had been waiting for that, to measure her confusion. "Is Lena Crouch dead?" she asked before he could question her.

"No, she'll be all right."

A weight lifted then and the lie came easy. "Well, she's the only one can tell you about Charlene."

He didn't find that a satisfactory answer. But the next moment they were diverted by the simultaneous arrival of the bus driver—not Will Taggart—who came running across Main Street, and Thelma Crouch, whose housedress and cane appeared on the blackened porch of the Surfside.

"She's been looking for you," the driver said, elbowing past Charlie when he got to the bus. "C'mon, get off, I'm late."

Alicia realized Charlene would know she'd told the name, and wanted to apologize, or say something, to tell her . . . "Please would you give Lena this for me?" She rolled the yellow elastic off her wrist, leaving herself only the brown. But one would be enough if she ever decided to comb her hair again. She held it out to him.

Charlie Lovall wasn't pleased with the errand. He took the little round thing and stood looking at it, making everyone wait as usual while he made his decision. Then Miss Thelma called from the porch. He stepped down.

They started immediately and went fast. At Norton's Bus Stop Café-Bar several passengers boarded, one with a lot of luggage. While it was stowed in the hatch at the side of the bus, Alicia had time to get coffee for Fay and juice and a piece of homemade cake for herself. Fay ate half the cake but Alicia didn't even care. It was always a good sign when Fay got hungry.

In fact Fay relaxed then, and put her seat back, and lay with her eyes closed. Tired, she looked beautiful as ever. Fine Fay. "At least she's alive," Charlene had said. Well she certainly was that, a large breathing mound in a Mexican shawl. Looking at her, Alicia recalled when soft was Mommy, remembered her whole body cradled on Fay's breasts. Then she sat staring down at her own, thinking of Gary's hands on them, and children on them, and again how big they might get. Popcorn titties, with a child asleep on them. And a rubber ass. She laughed to herself, surprised to find the idea didn't upset her this morning, she felt calm. Thinking about it, being a Polaminican how could she ever be exactly like Fay, or even like Mary Ann for that matter? Being a Polaminican meant she would *have* to be fast. You had to keep on your toes—it was a built-in situation.

The bus droned along in the Sunday quiet. At one point they stopped for a light on a street that followed the shore. Alicia looked out the window. In outline the coast was like a map of America, like the one she saw often, outside the social studies room near the gym. She put herself on the bulge that was New Jersey, conscious once more of having traveled in America, to a weird hick town. With hicks in it, she thought again. Even a mixed hick in it, she thought, giggling. She still didn't really understand Charlene's position but she wondered if there were others like her, and whether they were all crazy because of it. But surely some were okay, and she imagined herself crossing the map, from state to state, to find them. For what purpose she had no idea. To make trouble? To be friends? All she knew was she couldn't wait to tell the story in the yard.

After a while, when they had left the coast and were on the highway, she climbed over Fay and took a vacant seat across the aisle, and let the back of the seat down as far as it would go. She was stretched out like this, dozing, when the bus made a fast cloverleaf turn and then stopped. She sat up quickly, afraid they'd arrived. But they were only at the tunnel. The tollbooth attendant's hair, carefully corn-rowed, ended in delicate braided loops. Alicia raised a self-conscious hand to her head. Every day the possibilities increased.

About the author

Hettie Jones was born in Brooklyn, New York. She is the author of *Big Star Fallin' Mama: Five Women in Black Music* and lives with her daughters in New York City.